FROM THE PAGES OF *NARRATIVE OF THE LIFE OF FREDERICK DOUGLASS, AN AMERICAN SLAVE*

I am going away to the Great House Farm!
O, yea! O, yea! O!

(page 25)

I have sometimes thought that the mere hearing of those songs [of the slaves] would do more to impress some minds with the horrible character of slavery, than the reading of whole volumes of philosophy on the subject could do. . . . To those songs I trace my first glimmering conception of the dehumanizing character of slavery. I can never get rid of that conception. Those songs still follow me, to deepen my hatred of slavery, and quicken my sympathies for my brethren in bonds.

(page 26)

From my earliest recollection, I date the entertainment of a deep conviction that slavery would not always be able to hold me within its foul embrace; and in the darkest hours of my career in slavery, this living word of faith and spirit of hope departed not from me, but remained like ministering angels to cheer me through the gloom.

(page 39)

There were horses and men, cattle and women, pigs and children, all holding the same rank in the scale of being, and were all subjected to the same narrow examination. Silvery-headed age and sprightly youth, maids and matrons, had to undergo the same indelicate inspection. At this moment, I saw more clearly than ever the brutalizing effects of slavery upon both slave and slaveholder.

(page 49)

I was broken in body, soul, and spirit. My natural elasticity was crushed, my intellect languished, the disposition to read departed, the cheerful spark that lingered about my eye died; the dark night of slavery closed in upon me; and behold a man transformed into a brute! (page 63)

You have seen how a man was made a slave; you shall see how a slave was made a man. (page 64)

My long-crushed spirit rose, cowardice departed, bold defiance took its place; and I now resolved that, however long I might remain a slave in form, the day had passed forever when I could be a slave in fact. I did not hesitate to let it be known of me, that the white man who expected to succeed in whipping, must also succeed in killing me. (page 69)

I assert most unhesitatingly, that the religion of the south is a mere covering for the most horrid crimes,—a justifier of the most appalling barbarity,—a sanctifier of the most hateful frauds,—and a dark shelter under, which the darkest, foulest, grossest, and most infernal deeds of slaveholders find the strongest protection. Were I to be again reduced to the chains of slavery, next to that enslavement, I should regard being the slave of a religious master the greatest calamity that could befall me. For of all slaveholders with whom I have ever met, religious slaveholders are the worst. (page 72)

Let us render the tyrant no aid; let us not hold the light by which he can trace the footprints of our flying brother. (page 89)

NARRATIVE OF THE LIFE OF FREDERICK DOUGLASS, AN AMERICAN SLAVE

WRITTEN BY HIMSELF

*With an Introduction and Notes
by Robert O'Meally*

George Stade
Consulting Editorial Director

JB

BARNES & NOBLE CLASSICS
NEW YORK

JB

BARNES & NOBLE CLASSICS
NEW YORK

Published by Barnes & Noble Books
122 Fifth Avenue
New York, NY 10011

www.barnesandnoble.com/classics

Narrative of the Life of Frederick Douglass, an American Slave was
first published in 1845 by the Anti-Slavery Office.

Originally published in trade paperback format in 2003 by Barnes & Noble Classics
with new Introduction, Notes, Biography, Chronology, Inspired By,
Comments & Questions, and For Further Reading.
This hardcover format published in 2005.

Narrative of the Life of Frederick Douglass, an American Slave
ISBN-13: 978-1-59308-357-1
ISBN-10: 1-59308-357-2
LC Control Number 2004115105

Produced and published in conjunction with:
Fine Creative Media, Inc.
322 Eighth Avenue
New York, NY 10001

Michael J. Fine, President and Publisher

Printed in the United States of America

7 9 10 8 6

FREDERICK DOUGLASS

Frederick Augustus Washington Bailey was born a slave in Tuckahoe, Maryland, in February 1818. He became a leading abolitionist and women's rights advocate and one of the most influential public speakers and writers of the nineteenth century.

Frederick's mother, Harriet Bailey, was a slave; his father was rumored to be Aaron Anthony, manager for the large Lloyd plantation in St. Michaels, Maryland, and his mother's master. Frederick lived away from the plantation with his grandparents, Isaac and Betsey Bailey, until he was six years old, when he was sent to work for Anthony.

When Frederick was eight, he was sent to Baltimore as a houseboy for Hugh Auld, a shipbuilder related to the Anthony family through marriage. Auld's wife, Sophia, began teaching Frederick to read, but Auld, who believed that a literate slave was a dangerous slave, stopped the lessons. From that point on, Frederick viewed education and knowledge as a path to freedom. He continued teaching himself to read; in 1831 he bought a copy of *The Columbian Orator*, an anthology of great speeches, which he studied closely.

In 1833 Frederick was sent from Auld's relatively peaceful home back to St. Michaels to work in the fields. He was soon hired out to Edward Covey, a notorious "slave-breaker" who beat him brutally in an effort to crush his will. However, on an August afternoon in 1834, Frederick stood up to Covey and beat him in a fight. This was a turning point, Douglass has said, in his life as a slave; the experience reawakened his desire and drive for liberty.

After a failed escape attempt, Frederick was sent back to Baltimore, where he again worked for Hugh Auld, this time as a ship caulker. In Baltimore he met and fell in love with Anna Murray, a free black woman.

In 1838 Frederick Bailey escaped from slavery by using the papers of a free seaman. He traveled north to New York City, where Anna Murray soon joined him. Later that year, Frederick and Anna married and moved to New Bedford, Massachusetts. Though settled in the North, Frederick was a fugitive, technically still Auld's property. To protect himself, he became Frederick Douglass, a name inspired by a character in Sir Walter Scott's poem *Lady of the Lake*.

Douglass began speaking against slavery at abolitionist meetings and soon gained a reputation as a brilliant orator. In 1841 he began working full-time as an abolitionist lecturer, touring with one of the leading activists of the day, William Lloyd Garrison.

Douglass published his first autobiography, *Narrative of the Life of Frederick Douglass, an American Slave*, in 1845. The book became an immediate sensation and was widely read both in America and abroad. Its publication, however, jeopardized his freedom by exposing his true identity. To avoid capture as a fugitive slave, Douglass spent the next several years touring and speaking in England and Ireland. In 1846 two friends purchased his freedom. Douglass returned to America, an internationally renowned abolitionist and orator.

Douglass addressed the first Women's Rights Convention in Seneca Falls, New York, in 1848. This began his long association with the women's rights movement, including friendships with such well-known suffragists as Susan B. Anthony and Elizabeth Cady Stanton.

During the mid-1840s Douglass began to break ideologically from William Lloyd Garrison. Whereas Garrison's abolitionist sentiments were based in moral exhortation, Douglass was coming to believe that change would occur through political means. He became increasingly involved in antislavery politics with the Liberty and Free-Soil Parties. In 1847 Douglass established and edited the politically oriented, antislavery newspaper the *North Star*.

During the Civil War, President Lincoln called upon Douglass to advise him on emancipation issues. In addition, Douglass worked hard to secure the right of blacks to enlist; when the Fifty-fourth Massachusetts Volunteers was established as the first black regiment, he traveled throughout the North recruiting volunteers.

Douglass's governmental involvement extended far beyond Lincoln's tenure. He was consulted by the next five presidents and served as secretary of the Santo Domingo Commission (1871), marshal of the District of Columbia (1877–1881), recorder of deeds for the District of Columbia (1881–1886), and minister to Haiti (1889–1891). A year before his death Douglass delivered an important speech, "The Lessons of the Hour," a denunciation of lynchings in the United States.

On February 20, 1895, Frederick Douglass died of a heart attack. His death triggered an outpouring of grief and mourning; black schools in Washington, D.C., closed for a day, and thousands of children were taken to the Metropolitan African Methodist Episcopal Church to view his open casket. In his third autobiography, Douglass succinctly and aptly summarized his life; writing that he had "lived several lives in one: first, the life of slavery; secondly, the life of a fugitive from slavery; thirdly, the life of comparative freedom; fourthly, the life of conflict and battle; and fifthly, the life of victory, if not complete, at least assured."

TABLE OF CONTENTS

THE WORLD OF FREDERICK DOUGLASS AND *NARRATIVE OF THE LIFE OF FREDERICK DOUGLASS, AN AMERICAN SLAVE*

1818 In February Frederick Douglass is born Frederick Augustus Washington Bailey in Tuckahoe, Maryland. His mother, Harriet Bailey, is a slave; his father's identity is unknown, though many believe he was Douglass's white master, Aaron Anthony. Frederick is sent to be raised by his grandparents, Betsey and Isaac Bailey.

1824 Six-year-old Frederick is sent to St. Michaels, Maryland, to work on the Lloyd plantation, managed by Aaron Anthony.

1826 Frederick's mother dies. He is sent to Baltimore to work for Hugh Auld, a shipbuilder and the brother of Thomas Auld, Anthony's son-in-law. Frederick's job is to look after Auld's son, Tommy, and to work as a houseboy for Auld's wife, Sophia.

1827 Sophia Auld begins to teach Frederick to read, but her husband stops the lessons. Frederick continues learning on his own.

1831 Having saved fifty cents, he purchases a copy of *The Columbian Orator*, an anthology of great speeches from leading orators throughout history, on such issues as liberty, equality, and justice.

1833 In March Frederick is sent back to St. Michaels to work for Thomas Auld.

1834 In January he is hired out as a field hand to Edward Covey, a professional "slave-breaker" who beats intransigent slaves into submission. After nearly eight months, Frederick stands up to Covey and beats him in a fight.

1835 Frederick is hired out to William Freeland as a field hand. He opens a Sunday school for young blacks and begins teaching them to read and write.

1836 Frederick and several other of Covey's slaves attempt to escape, but are caught and imprisoned. Thomas Auld takes him out of prison and sends him back to Baltimore, where Hugh Auld trains him to become a ship caulker.

1837   He meets and falls in love with Anna Murray, a free black woman.

1838   On September 3 Frederick successfully escapes from slavery using a sailor's "protection papers" (documents certifying the bearer is a free seaman). He arrives in New York City on September 4 and, to avoid recapture, changes his name to Frederick Johnson. Anna Murray joins him in New York and they marry on September 15. They move to New Bedford, Massachusetts. Frederick again changes his name, this time to Frederick Douglass, after a character in *Lady of the Lake* (1810), a historical poem by Sir Walter Scott.

1839   In New Bedford Douglass works as a day laborer and begins speaking at abolitionist meetings. His first child, Rosetta, is born on June 24.

1840   The Douglass's son Lewis is born.

1841   In August Douglass travels to Nantucket to attend a meeting of the Massachusetts Anti-Slavery Society; he meets the abolitionist William Lloyd Garrison, president of the American Anti-Slavery Society and editor of the well-known abolitionist paper *The Liberator*. Impressed by Douglass's eloquent and powerful speech, Garrison employs him as an antislavery speaker.

1842   A second son, Frederick, is born. Douglass begins traveling in New England, New York, and elsewhere around the North as an abolitionist speaker. He tells his personal story and attacks both slavery and northern racism. He and his family move to Lynn, Massachusetts, where Anna finds work in a shoe factory.

1844   Another son, Charles Remond, is born.

1845   In May Douglass publishes *Narrative of the Life of Frederick Douglass, an American Slave*. The book is well received and widely publicized. However, its publication exposes his identity, and fearing capture as a fugitive slave, he leaves the country. He begins traveling through England and Ireland, speaking against slavery.

1846 On December 5, 1846, friends purchase Douglass's freedom from Thomas Auld.

1847 Douglass returns to the United States in the spring; he and his family move to Rochester, New York. On December 3 he founds an antislavery newspaper, the *North Star*, which he continues to edit until 1860 (the paper's name becomes *Frederick Douglass's Paper* in 1851).

1848 Douglass attends and speaks at the first Women's Rights Convention in Seneca Falls, New York, beginning his long association with the women's rights movement.

1849 His daughter, Annie, is born.

1850 Douglass becomes part of the Underground Railroad network, using his home as a hiding place for fugitive slaves traveling north.

1851 Douglass definitively breaks with Garrison, disagreeing over the issue of moral exhortation (which Garrison favored) versus political action (Douglass's preference) as the major tool for eliminating slavery.

1852 On July 4 Douglass delivers an impassioned speech about the meaning of freedom and slavery in a republic and about continuing hypocrisy and injustice.

1855 His second autobiography, *My Bondage and My Freedom*, is published.

1859 Abolitionist John Brown tries to enlist Douglass's support in a raid to liberate slaves at Harpers Ferry, Virginia (now West Virginia); Douglass refuses, believing it to be a doomed effort. On October 16 Brown goes through with his raid and is caught; he is later tried and hanged for treason. Because of his association with Brown, Douglass flees to England.

1860 Douglass's daughter, Annie, dies and he returns to Rochester. He campaigns for Abraham Lincoln, who is elected president in November.

1861 The Civil War begins. Douglass is a vocal proponent of the right of blacks to enlist and an aggressive propagandist for the Union cause.

1863 On January 1 President Abraham Lincoln issues the Emancipation Proclamation, freeing all slaves in Confederate areas not held by Union troops. The first black regiment, the Fifty-fourth Massachusetts Volunteers, is assembled. Two of Douglass's sons, Lewis and Charles, are among the recruits. Douglass travels throughout the North and recruits more than 100 members for the regiment; but he stops recruiting after a few months because of rampant discrimination against the black soldiers.

1864 Douglass is called to the White House to discuss strategies for emancipation.

1865 He attends the White House reception following Lincoln's second inauguration. The Civil War ends on April 9, and on April 14 Lincoln is assassinated. In December Congress ratifies the Thirteenth Amendment to the U.S. Constitution, abolishing slavery.

1866 Douglass supports Republican Reconstruction plans. He is part of a delegation that meets with President Andrew Johnson (who harbors Confederate sympathies) to push for black suffrage.

1868– Douglass campaigns for Ulysses S. Grant, who wins the
1870 presidency in 1868. On March 30, 1870, Congress passes the Fifteenth Amendment, which gives blacks the right to vote. Douglass's support for this measure, which does not include women, causes a temporary rift with women's rights supporters.

1871 Grant appoints Douglass secretary of a commission to Santo Domingo.

1872 The Douglass's Rochester home is destroyed by fire; no one is injured, but many of Douglass's important papers are lost. The family moves to Washington, D.C.

1874 Douglass is named president of Freedman's Savings and Trust Company, a bank that had been founded to encourage blacks to save and invest their money. The bank is on the verge of collapse when Douglass takes it over, and it soon closes. A newspaper Douglass had purchased in 1870—the *New National Era*—also closes.

1877 President Rutherford B. Hayes appoints Douglass marshal of the District of Columbia, a post he holds until 1881. Douglass returns to St. Michaels, Maryland, and meets with his former owner Auld, who is dying.

1881 President James Garfield appoints Douglass recorder of deeds for the District of Columbia, a post he holds until 1886. Douglass publishes his third autobiographical volume, *Life and Times of Frederick Douglass*.

1882 His wife, Anna, dies in August.

1884 Douglass causes something of a scandal when he marries his former secretary, Helen Pitts, who is white.

1889 President Benjamin Harrison appoints him minister and consul general to Haiti, a post he holds until 1891.

1894 Douglass delivers his last major speech, "The Lessons of the Hour," a denunciation of lynchings in the United States.

1895 On February 20 Frederick Douglass dies in Washington, D.C., of a heart attack. He is buried in Rochester beside his first wife and his daughter, Anna.

1988 On February 12 Douglass's home in Washington, D.C., is designated the Frederick Douglass National Historic Site.

INTRODUCTION

Crossing Over: Frederick Douglass's Run for Freedom

THE VERY FIRST TIME I assigned Frederick Douglass's *Narrative* was in the fall of 1972, in Boston, Massachusetts, when I was teaching a high school equivalency night-course for working adults. I remember the occasion well because one of the students complained to the school director that I was teaching hate. The class had met only once, and we had not yet discussed the book at all, so this student, a white nurse's aide in her late twenties, directed her protest against the fiery book itself, which she took to be an attack upon her and all white people in America.

In a peculiarly American turn of events, the director, who like me was an African American, happened also to be one of my friends and hallmates at Harvard, where we both were working on our doctorates. In the night-school's hallway, he told me about the complaint with a long, stern face, and then closed his office door so we could laugh until we nearly fell to the floor. "Ole Brother Douglass is still working them roots," he said, sliding into the vernacular once we could speak in private. "Go easy on the lady," he went on. "Gentle her into the twentieth century."

At that time Douglass was not considered a canonical American author, though he did sometimes turn up in surveys of nineteenth-century writing and in courses with titles like "The Negro in American Literature." The revolution in black literary studies was just beginning to catch fire; but still at Harvard, for example, there was no course in black literature offered at the graduate level, and the one such undergraduate course, in which I was a teaching assistant, was offered by a linguist through the Afro-American Studies Department. (It was an excellent course.) So it was not a shock that this young woman, a few years older than I and not yet a high school graduate, had never heard of Frederick Douglass. What was surprising was that this slender volume, with its antique figures of speech and rhetorical strategies (as well as literary structures that were so modern they seem to have influenced such revolutionaries in writing as Hemingway eighty years later) would strike her as so current in its potency that she wanted to swing back at it.

Part of the answer to the mystery of her response is that many of white Boston's citizenry in the early seventies were literally up in arms against the "forced desegregation" of schools and neighborhoods that had been as firmly closed to blacks and members of other groups considered unwelcome as were their counterparts in Mississippi or Alabama. No doubt my student was as unaccustomed to a black teacher as she was to a black author. (What on earth went through her mind when she discovered that the program director was black, too?!)

Does not this woman's bewildered anger indicate that although the *Narrative of the Life of Frederick Douglass, an American Slave* existed as a mightily effective political weapon, it is much more than a political weapon, which might have dulled over time? That it is also a work of art whose sentences, with their careful twists and balances and their unrelenting drive, continue to evoke a direct, visceral response? She may have felt the power of the book's stark, biblical last-first/first-last language: the reverse-English of a man belonging to the group counted last in the American social hierarchy but who nonetheless became a leader of his people—meaning (though my student did not realize it) not just blacks but all Americans and indeed all who love freedom.

With his *Narrative*, Douglass succeeded in offering his readers, and eventually also historians of American life, an unassailably reliable record of slavery from the viewpoint of one who had been enslaved. (It is important to realize that Douglass could not afford to exaggerate or get any name or detail wrong lest the proponents of slavery leap to declare him a fraud, as they were eager to do in the case of such an accomplished former slave.) But the book also brilliantly performed the aesthetic task of a work of art in depicting how it feels to be a human locked in a struggle against tyrannical odds for freedom and culture; a man seeking a place in a world where no place looks like home. In other words, yes, Douglass *was* still working those roots.

Douglass's book lures its reader through the unrelenting power of its narrative line—perhaps literature's most irresistible force. It is driven by impulses evidently built into the reflex and bone structure of *Homo sapiens*, the animal that wants a story. Douglass shapes his story to resonate with certain mythic patterns in the modern world. The Douglass of this narrative is a poor lost boy a long way from home, one who has no home to miss or to which he can return. With no place and nothing to call his own, no name, no birthday, no mother to whom he feels closely attached, no father to nurture or even to acknowledge him, this scarred and battered slave boy is an exile in the land of his birth. What Douglass does not invoke is a sense of special honor or privilege based on lineage. He knows little about his past—either of his unknown white father's side or his mother's—and, even if he did, could make no claim to either side. This aligns him with many of America's dispossessed immigrants, black and nonblack, who either were brought to the New World as slaves or who came here under dire economic distress. Having virtually nothing more than his own health, strength, will, and a strong sense that God's mysterious power is on his side, Douglass's task in the new land will be to improvise—that is, not just to find but to help create—a new way of life, a home at last.

What separates Douglass's quest for improvement from, say, those of dime-store Horatio Alger heroes of a generation later, is that his will to free himself is so directly related to his will to help others free themselves. The climax of his narrative is not just his own escape and, crucially, his marriage, which brings the beginnings of a new family and community; he also finds redeeming work as an activist in the abolition movement, and, as it turns out, as an artist. His identity, in other words, is not that of the bourgeois individual who puts himself first; instead it depends deeply on his providential fellowship with an activist community that gives his own being its most profound meaning. From the first "I was born . . ." to the final ringing words addressed to "the millions of my brethren in bonds," Douglass speaks for that community and for a sense of ideal community that has implications for the nation. As the writer Albert Murray has observed, compared with other American icons seeking freedom—Davy Crockett or Daniel Boone, for example—the case of Douglass stands out. "Nobody was chasing Daniel Boone!" "Not even such justly canonized Founding Fathers as Benjamin Franklin and

Thomas Jefferson represent a more splendid image and pattern for the contemporary American citizen," writes Murray. "On balance, not even Abraham Lincoln was a more heroic embodiment of the American as self-made man. After all, Lincoln like Franklin and Jefferson was born free."*

Douglass was an American improviser whose mighty task was to have the courage, simply, *to be*—an achievement that by no means could be taken for granted in a society that defined him as a domestic animal, a piece of property to buy, work, rent, inherit, or sell. The simple assertion of Douglass's selfhood begins quietly, on the title page, with the announcement that this *Narrative of the Life of Frederick Douglass, an American Slave* was *"written by himself."* In direct opposition to the southern slave codes, which he repeatedly mocks and derides in his *Narrative*, Douglass has garnered sufficient literacy to get his story down in black and white. And lest anyone miss the connection between his achievement of authorial power and his fight against slavery's hardships, he declares, "My feet have been so cracked with the frost, that the pen with which I am writing might be laid in the gashes" (p. 36).

The two stirringly oratorical introductory notes by Douglass's white brothers in the movement, William Lloyd Garrison and Wendell Phillips, serve to guarantee the authenticity of the narrative that follows. But Douglass is the one in control of his story, its author and authority asserting the truth of what he says not through the presence of white guarantors but through the power of his own language as a persuasive, sometimes poetic writer whose voice and witness we trust. His book is a shining example of what Robert Stepto has brilliantly termed a "self-authenticating narrative";† it is a book whose proof of truth-value lies precisely in its own language.

Douglass's *Narrative* presents its hero as a reasonable and feeling

---

The Omni-Americans: New Perspectives on Black Experience and American Culture (New York: Outerbridge and Dienstfrey, 1970), pp. 19–20.

†"Narration, Authentication, and Authorial Control in Frederick Douglass' Narrative of 1845." In *Afro-American Literature: The Reconstruction of Instruction*, edited by Dexter Fisher and Robert B. Stepto (New York: Modern Language Association of America, 1929), pp. 178–191. It should be noted that this argument about Douglass's authorial control is Robert Stepto's, from the article just mentioned.

human being, a man with a soul. But it also argues, implicitly, for the whole slave community as worthy members of the world community of culture-makers, all denials of their humanity to the contrary (that is, all the scenes of the slaves herded, fed, and beaten like animals). Douglass is a maker of literature and history; the black community writ large has created cultural forms people can use to survive the pit of slavery and to help rebuild a modern world.

For one thing, African Americans created the slave songs—the musical fountain from which virtually all modern American music, including the blues, has sprung. In terms echoed by W. E. B. Du Bois nearly sixty years later,* Douglass describes the rich mix of feeling in the songs of sorrow sung by slaves as they took off for the Great House Farm:

> While on their way, they would make the dense old woods, for miles around, reverberate with their wild songs, revealing at once the highest joy and the deepest sadness. They would compose and sing as they went along, consulting neither time nor tune. The thought that came up, came out—if not in the word, in the sound;—and as frequently in the one as in the other. They would sometimes sing the most pathetic sentiment in the most rapturous tone, and the most rapturous sentiment in the most pathetic tone. . . . They would sing, as a chorus, to words which to many would seem unmeaning jargon, but which, nevertheless, were full of meaning to themselves. I have sometimes thought that the mere hearing of those songs would do more to impress some minds with the horrible character of slavery, than the reading of whole volumes of philosophy on the subject could do (pp. 25–26).

It is true that Douglass is concerned about the dangers of misreading this music. He concludes his eloquent discussion of the slave's songs with a warning that they could easily be misunderstood. Douglass:

> I did not, when a slave, understand the deep meaning of those rude and apparently incoherent songs. I was myself within the circle; so

---

***The Souls of Black Folk* (Chicago: A. C. McClurg, 1903).

that I neither saw nor heard as those without might see and hear. They told a tale of woe which was then altogether beyond my feeble comprehension; they were tones loud, long, and deep; they breathed the prayer and complaint of souls boiling over with the bitterest anguish. Every tone was a testimony against slavery, and a prayer to God for deliverance from chains. The hearing of those wild notes always depressed my spirit, and filled me with ineffable sadness. I have frequently found myself in tears while hearing them. The mere recurrence to those songs, even now, afflicts me; and while I am writing these lines, an expression of feeling has already found its way down my cheek. To those songs I trace my first glimmering conception of the dehumanizing character of slavery. I can never get rid of that conception. Those songs still follow me, to deepen my hatred of slavery, and quicken my sympathies for my brethren in bonds. If any one wishes to be impressed with the soul-killing effects of slavery, let him go to Colonel Lloyd's plantation, and, on allowance-day, place himself in the deep pine woods, and there let him, in silence, analyze the sounds that shall pass through the chambers of his soul,—and if he is not thus impressed, it will only be because "there is no flesh in his obdurate heart" (p. 26).

Aware that he himself had misread the meanings of this music, Douglass warns his reader against missing the note of sadness and implied protest—against the "soul-killing effects of slavery"—embedded in the music. Addressing in particular his sympathetic northern white reader, he writes:

I have often been utterly astonished, since I came to the north, to find persons who could speak of the singing, among slaves, as evidence of their contentment and happiness. It is impossible to conceive of a greater mistake. Slaves sing most when they are most unhappy. The songs of the slave represent the sorrows of his heart; and he is relieved by them, only as an aching heart is relieved by its tears. At least, such is my experience. I have often sung to drown my sorrow, but seldom to express my happiness. Crying for joy, and singing for joy, were alike uncommon to me while in the jaws of slavery. The singing of a man cast away upon a desolate island might be as appropriately considered as evidence of contentment and happiness, as the singing of a slave;

the songs of the one and of the other are prompted by the same emotion (pp. 26–27).

On this question of reading and misreading, Robert Stepto has written brilliantly that Douglass's quest can be focused into two specific terms: He sought *freedom*, and he sought *literacy*.* Make no mistake about it: His was a physical fight, against the slave-breaker Edward Covey and others, and a literal struggle to remove his body from the South, where slavery was legal. What fascinates me here is the vital connection between Douglass's ongoing physical struggle and his flaming determination to learn how to write and read—including the ability to read such cultural manifestations of slavery as the slave songs.

In the compressed and powerful chapter VI, Douglass describes overhearing Mr. Auld, his new owner, warning his wife against teaching the slave boy Frederick his ABCs. He told her "that it was unlawful, as well as unsafe, to teach a slave to read." Further, he declared these infamous words:

"If you give a nigger an inch, he will take an ell. A nigger should know nothing but to obey his master—to do as he is told to do. Learning would *spoil* the best nigger in the world. . . . If you teach that nigger . . . how to read, there would be no keeping him. It would forever unfit him to be a slave. He would at once become unmanageable, and of no value to his master. As to himself, it could do him no good, but a great deal of harm. It would make him discontented and unhappy" (pp. 40–41).

Douglass's recollected response to his master's words is mythic:

These words sank deep into my heart, stirred up sentiments within that lay slumbering, and called into existence an entirely new train of thought. It was a new and special revelation, explaining dark and mys-

---

*"Teaching Afro-American Literature: Survey or Tradition." In *Afro-American Literature: The Reconstruction of Instruction*, pp. 8–24. Here Stepto argues that this quest for freedom and literacy informs African-American literature as a coherent literary tradition and "pre-generic myth," that is, a set of impulses and values antedating the creation of literary forms as such.

terious things, with which my youthful understanding had struggled, but struggled in vain. I now understood what had been to me a most perplexing difficulty—to wit, the white man's power to enslave the black man. It was a grand achievement, and I prized it highly. *From that moment, I understood the pathway from slavery to freedom.* . . . In learning to read, I owe almost as much to the bitter opposition of my master, as to the kindly aid of my mistress. I acknowledge the benefit of both (p. 41, emphasis mine).

As a reader and writer, Douglass could read the newspaper as well as books that happened his way—so that he could better understand his predicament and possible solutions to it; he also was literally able to write himself a false pass (in his first failed escape attempt, he also wrote passes for his co-conspirators), which was crucial to his eventual plan to get out of the slave South. Freedom and literacy—tightly bound strands in the fabric of Douglass's mythic quest. Further, as we have seen, Douglass's quest for literacy involved not merely the technical ability to read and write but also the skill to "read" the people, places, situations, and expressive forms around him with deeper and deeper understanding. He wrote his way to freedom not just with a pass but also by articulating new terms for living: "to dream of vast horizons of the soul," as Langston Hughes has put it, to "make our world anew."*

Along with the complex songs, black Americans also created a cycle of trickster tales—yarns about Brer Rabbits, Brother Johns, and others living by their wits in the briar patch of the United States. As he tells in this *Narrative*—as if tempered by these slave stories—Douglass learns, by degrees, that he is born into a world controlled by slave-owners whose power is nearly absolute, that as an American slave he lives in what might be called *the world of the trickster*, and that to survive he must learn the games of trickery by which he is being kept.

In the realm of the tales told by black Americans, and by many other groups around the world, the trickster is a paradoxical charac-

---

*From Langston Hughes's poem "To You," *Amsterdam News* (January 30, 1965), p. 22; reprinted in *The Collected Poems of Langston Hughes*, edited by Arnold Rampersad (New York: Vintage, 1995), p. 546.

ter, both wish-fulfillment hero and horrific villain. The Brer Rabbit of black American tales collected "in the field," both in the nineteenth century of Frederick Douglass and through the mid-twentieth century not far from our own times, is precisely such a figure of double purposes: admired for his ability to overturn the powerful with cleverness and stealth, and yet hated for his insatiable greed and selfishness. Conditioned, perhaps, by the Brer Rabbits on television (in a sense Bugs Bunny is a latter-day Brer Rabbit) and in the movies (every other American over the age of fifty has seen Walt Disney's 1946 film *Song of the South*, with its fast, fluffy wish-fulfillment hero Brer Rabbit), we tend to remember our admiration for his good-humored ability to dance away from traps set for him by the Elmer Fudds of the world.

In the context of trickster behavior in Douglass's *Narrative*, though, we must not forget the other Brer Rabbit: the one who eats the food of all the other animals, the one who cares nothing for the community but lives only for private pleasure, the monster who will deceive, punish, and kill even his own family to gain and maintain personal power. The trickster is he, and sometimes she, whose tokens almost always take the same forms: sex (not love, but pure physical pleasure through domination), food, and money. As Robert Bone has argued so well,* the Brer Rabbit tales that circulated orally among the slaves had two purposes: to teach the small but clever bunny's survival skills, required if the weak were to stay alive under the dominion of the powerful; and also, crucially, to serve as cautionary tales exposing the slave-holder (and those like him) as a kind of Brer Rabbit run wild and somehow elected to the presidency. It is this latter trickster as great white monster against which Douglass first learns to brace himself.

In the *Narrative*'s first chapter, Douglass lets his readers know that he lives in this dangerous trickster's den by describing the extraordinarily cruel beating of his beautiful Aunt Hester. As a baby and toddler living with his grandmother on the outskirts of the plantation, Douglass had been protected from the workaday life of the slave. But

---

Down Home: Origins of the Afro-American Short Story, New York: Columbia University Press, 1975.

now, moved to the plantation itself, he witnesses the first evidence of his true situation as he sees Hester under the lash. Jealous that she has been spending time with another man, a slave named Ned Roberts, Mr. Anthony, the master, strips Aunt Hester from neck to waist, fastens her hands with a rope hooked to the ceiling, and slashes her naked back with heavy rawhide. "And soon the warm, red blood (amid heart-rending shrieks from her, and horrid oaths from him) came dripping to the floor," writes Douglass, who was "so terrified and horror-stricken at the sight, that I hid myself in a closet, and dared not venture out till long after the bloody transaction was over. I expected it would be my turn next" (p. 21).

This terrible scene initiates the boy Douglass into the treacherous and chaotic world of the trickster in power. If in this nineteenth-century world of southern chivalry, a young black woman had no protection from raw, lawless brutality, how could Douglass not assume that there were no laws or limits at all, that indeed his turn would come next?—particularly when the perpetrator of the arbitrary violence seemed "to take," in Douglass's words, "great pleasure" in the act of whipping. All of her human responses, voluntary and involuntary, made the situation worse: "The louder she screamed, the harder he whipped; and where the blood ran fastest, there he whipped longest. He would whip her to make her scream, and whip her to make her hush; and not until overcome by fatigue, would he cease to swing the blood-clotted cowskin" (p. 20). This terrifying scene, says Douglass, "was the blood-stained gate, the entrance to the hell of slavery, through which I was about to pass" (p. 20).

In his *Narrative* Douglass delivers a modicum of justice to the sadistic Anthony by the sheer act of describing his brutality and then exposing the baseness of his motives. As we shall see, Douglass the slave has learned to beware Brer Rabbit in master's clothing as well as to become enough of a trickster himself to survive the trickster's lair. And listen for the trickster-like aggressive laughter of Douglass the writer, who describes, with a blue-hot rage barely concealed under the language's deadpan surfaces, the man who beat his mother's sister: "I have had two masters. My first master's name was Anthony. I do not remember his first name. He was generally called Captain Anthony—a title which, I presume, he acquired by sailing a craft on the Chesapeake Bay" (p. 19). In other words, this miserable man was no more a legitimate captain or leader of any kind than any other pretentious little man, any other human *ant*-ony, or whatever his name was.

Later Douglass would level his verbal guns on Captain Auld, presumably another bogusly titled figure, describing him as so emphatically mean that "the leading trait in his character was meanness; and if there were any other element in his nature, it was made subject to this. He was mean; and, like most other mean men, he lacked the ability to conceal his meanness." To top off his depiction of Auld as ridiculous—"incapable of managing his slaves either by force, fear, or fraud"—Douglass says, "he might have passed for a lion, but for his ears" (p. 55). The man pretended a lion's power, but still he looked foolish: He had "his ears." Were they Brer Rabbit's ears?

This verbal aggressiveness is also seen in Douglass's description of Mr. Severe: "rightly named. . . . His presence [where slaves were at work] made it both the field of blood and of blasphemy. From the rising till the going down of the sun, he was cursing, raving, cutting, and slashing among the slaves of the field, in the most frightful manner" (p. 24). And of Mr. Gore, whom we presume also to have been "rightly named," at home as he was in the realm of cruelty to slaves: "He was just the man for such a place, and it was just the place for such a man. . . . Though a young man, he indulged in no jokes, said no funny words, seldom smiled. His words were in perfect keeping with his looks, and his looks were in perfect keeping with his words. . . . He spoke but to command, and commanded but to be obeyed; he dealt sparingly with his words, and bountifully with his whip, never using the former where the latter would answer as well" (pp. 32–33).

Without question the clearest evidence that Douglass saw the slave-holders as grim tricksters-in-command comes in his descriptions of the slave-breaker Edward Covey. Douglass reports that among themselves the slaves called Covey "the snake." Was Covey thus given the name of another trickster from the realm of animal tales? In careful language, Douglass describes how "the snake"

had the faculty of making us feel that he was ever present with us. This he did by surprising us. He seldom approached the spot where we were at work openly, if he could do it secretly. He always aimed at taking us by surprise. . . . When we were at work in the cornfield, he

would sometimes crawl on his hands and knees to avoid detection,
and all at once he would rise nearly in our midst, and scream out, "Ha,
ha! Come, come! Dash on, dash on!" This being his mode of attack, it
was never safe to stop a single minute. His comings were like a thief
in the night. He appeared to us as being ever at hand. He was under
every tree, behind every stump, in every bush, and at every window,
on the plantation. He would sometimes mount his horse, as if bound
to St. Michael's, a distance of seven miles, and in half an hour afterwards you would see him coiled up in the corner of the wood-fence,
watching every motion of the slaves (p. 61).

On another day Covey would pretend to give frank instructions in connection with a long trip he was taking; but then, "before he would get
half way thither, he would turn short and crawl into a fence-corner, or
behind some tree, and there watch us till the going down of the sun."
    Lest anyone miss the point, Douglass tells his reader that "Covey's
forte consisted in his power to deceive. His life was devoted to planning and perpetrating the grossest deceptions. Every thing he possessed in the shape of learning or religion, he made conform to his
disposition to deceive. He seemed to think himself equal to deceiving the Almighty" (p. 61). This white trickster, lying in wait for po-
tential black tricksters, recalls the ruse of Douglass's former owner
Colonel Lloyd, whose plan to keep slaves out of his beautiful, fruit-
filled garden was a variation on the rabbit's strategy in the tale of Brer
Rabbit and the tar-baby. Lloyd put tar on the fence around the garden, "after which, if a slave was caught with any tar upon his person,
it was deemed sufficient proof that he had either been into the garden, or had tried to get in. In either case, he was severely whipped by
the chief gardener" (p. 28). The other side of this, of course, is that
doubtless the slaves were working just as hard to avoid the tar, while
getting the fruit, as Lloyd was to keep them out of his garden in the
first place. Trickster versus trickster.
    As with the names of Captain Anthony, Mr. Severe, and Mr.
Gore,* so with Covey's name, which, as with the others, Douglass

---

*And eventually his owner named Mr. Freeland, of whom Douglass would write: "I
began to want to live *upon free land* as well as *with Freeland*" (p. 76).

underscores for mockery by repeating it over and over again. According to Noah Webster's 1828 dictionary, the dictionary that would have been on Douglass's desk, "covey" is derived from the French noun *couvee*, meaning "brood" or "hatch of offspring," and the verb *cubare*, meaning "to lurk or lie hid"; the dictionary defines "covey" as: "1. a brood or hatch of birds; an old fowl with her brood of young," and "2. a company; a set." The modern *Oxford English Dictionary* specifies that a covey is "a family of partridges keeping together during the first season." As we consider Douglass's ongoing strategy of gaining elbow-room on these tricksters by deflating them with sharp, aggressive language, note his constant naming of Mr. Covey, whose pluralized moniker suggests, under the pressure of Douglass's insistent mockery, both the slave-driver's egotistical pretenses of omnipresence and Covey's secret identity not only as a snake but as "an old fowl" and lurking mother bird—this in a book all about the exigencies of true manhood.

This "Covey's" teenage charge, Douglass, ultimately refuses to recognize the slave-driver's legitimate authority; he turns the tables on Covey not only with artful language but also with physical force. In the highly charged terms of this encounter, Douglass's victory over Covey indicates more than one man's defeat of another. It is the boy David's defeat of mighty Goliath. The language also suggests the smashing by Frederick (soon to be renamed Douglass, after a storybook hero) of what might be called *a whole covey of Coveys*, of the system of American slavery itself, with its absurd pretensions of protecting and nurturing a black child-race in need of white "covey-ing." In Douglass's subtle but take-no-prisoners formulation, this absurd, brooding mother-partridge is nothing but a snake!

It was under Covey's brutal management that Douglass took seven-league boot-sized strides toward freedom. Again in mythic terms, Douglass describes how at first Covey's snaky brutality and interminable regimen of hard labor defeated his spirit. "A few months of this discipline tamed me," Douglass says. "Mr. Covey succeeded in breaking me. I was broken in body, soul, and spirit. My natural elasticity was crushed, my intellect languished, the disposition to read departed, the cheerful spark that lingered about my eye died; the dark night of slavery closed in upon me; and behold a man transformed

into a brute!" He was "sometimes prompted" to kill Covey and himself, "but was prevented by a combination of hope and fear" (p. 63).

Douglass describes his reversal of fortune in terms that are at once
mystical and deeply responsive to his hard-fought struggles in trick-
sterdom. In a now-famous passage, he apostrophizes the sparkling
Chesapeake Bay, "whose broad bosom was ever white with sails from
every quarter of the habitable globe" (p. 63), choosing terms that suggest a refusal of Covey's thorny hatch in favor of protection under the
majestic wings of the beautiful ships on the bay: "You are freedom's
swift-winged angels, that fly round the world," he calls to the winds.
"I am confined in bands of iron! O that I were free! O, that I were on
one of your gallant decks, and under your protecting wing!" With
these angels of freedom before his eyes, he resolves to risk his life to
get away. "I have only one life to lose. I had as well be killed running
as die standing. . . . Try it? Yes! God helping me, I will." He rounds
off this paragraph of mystical revelation and conviction quite appropriately, with a quote from the spirituals: "There is a better day coming."

Douglass resolves never again to be beaten by Covey, or anyone
else, without a fight. In anticipation of his showdown with Covey,
while watching the ships on Chesapeake Bay he says, "You have seen
how a man was made a slave; you shall see how a slave was made a
man." By framing the sentence in this way, Douglass uses the diago-
nal turn of phrase that we saw in his previous descriptions of Auld
and Gore (for example, "just the man for such a place, just the place
for such a man"): a strategy of Latin and Greek speeches called *chiasmus*, a verbal crisscrossing in which the order of words in the first
clause of a sentence is inverted in the second. (John F. Kennedy used
chiasmus when he said, "Ask not what your country can do for you,
ask what you can do for your country.")

I linger on chiasmus because this figure of speech, this verbal reversal, is important to the structure and meaning of Douglass's whole
book, and to the meaning of Douglass's reversal of fortunes, his turning of the tables on his trickster-adversaries. Indeed, as we shall see,
we may describe this as a double-double-cross, as one kind of trickster reverses the fortunes of another. For Douglass's mission was not
merely to write a nicely balanced set of sentences but to undermine
and reverse a system of power relations: to show the master as slave

(to liquor, to power, to sadism), the professed Christian as hypocrite, the weak as strong, the slave as free—from one point of view, ironically freer than the master. As Henry Louis Gates, Jr., has observed, this pattern of reverse language begins in the first pages of the narrative,* where Douglass repeatedly describes the very dark skin of his mother, whom he seemed to see, as he repeats, only *at night*, emphasizing the darkness drawn in opposition to the stark daylight world of white control. Eventually—in a broad pattern of chiasmus—the dark people enjoying only flashes of family togetherness and control in the night will take control of their daylight hours, too, as their fortunes turn like a chiasmus-reversed sentence: a sea-change at 180-degrees, toward freedom.†

Back at work after his revelation at Chesapeake Bay, Douglass falls sick, and as punishment Covey beats him severely. Failing to find protection from his (il)legal owner Master Thomas, who had rented Douglass to Covey, Douglass returns to Covey; but when Covey runs out to beat him again, Douglass runs away again to hide in the woods. "My behavior," says Douglass, "was altogether unaccountable." What follows is a highly significant scene in which Douglass, on the run but without resources to attempt a run for freedom, falls in with fellow-slave Sandy Jenkins, and seeks his advice concerning what to do next. "I found Sandy an old adviser," writes Douglass. Sandy Jenkins's advice is surprising in the context of Christianity but not in the context of Douglass's ongoing battle against the forces of tricksterism.

---

*"Binary Oppositions in Chapter One of *Narrative of the Life of Frederick Douglass, an American Slave Written by Himself.*" In *Afro-American Literature: The Reconstruction of Instruction*, pp. 212–232.

†In "Binary Oppositions," Gates notes a pattern of oppositions in Douglass's first chapter that has even more far-reaching implications, encompassing "the animal, the mother, the slave, the night, the earth, matrilinear succession, and nature opposed to relation of the human being, the father, the master, the daylight, the heavens, patrilinear succession, and culture. Douglass, in short, opposes the absolute and the eternal to the mortal and the finite. Our list, certainly, could be expanded to include oppositions between spiritual/material, aristocratic/base, civilized/barbaric, sterile/fertile, enterprise/sloth, force/principle, fact/imagination, linear/cyclical, thinking/feeling, rational/irrational, chivalry/cowardice, grace/brutishness, pure/cursed, and human/beastly" (pp. 225–226).

He told me, with great solemnity, I must go back to Covey; but that before I went, I must go with him into another part of the woods, where there was a certain *root*, which, if I would take some of it with me, carrying it *always on my right side*, would render it impossible for Mr. Covey, or any other white man, to whip me. He said he had carried it for years; and since he had done so, he had never received a blow, and never expected to while he carried it. I at first rejected the idea, that the simple carrying of a root in my pocket would have any such effect as he had said, and was not disposed to take it; but Sandy impressed the necessity with much earnestness, telling me it could do no harm if it did no good. To please him, I at length took the root, and, according to his direction, carried it upon my right side (pp. 67–68).

The best gloss for this scene has been provided by the writer Toni Morrison, who argues that Sandy embodies an ancestral tradition of root workers and doctors traceable back through African-American religio-medicinal practices of the South and the Caribbean to the continent of Africa. Further, Sandy (whose name seems to reinforce his identity as a man of the spirit and of the earth—perhaps of the seashore) offers a "safe space" and encouragements that serve to reconnect Douglass with a sense of a black community that cares about him, and which has ways of its own that are beyond the watch and guard of slavery and slave-holders, with their officially sanctioned practices and epistemologies.* Sandy's identity as an "old adviser" married to a free woman suggests possibilities of freedom and family for Douglass, too. Slavery has been a cauldron of family separation; but here are a wise man and family unit to prove, as Douglass had announced at Chesapeake Bay, a better day coming. Here, too, is hope that the powers of the black world—the dark mother, the night, the root from the ground now secretly held in the pocket—will invade and reverse the bleak, blaring bright world overseen by the likes of Covey, a snake in the sun watching and waiting to attack.

---

*Toni Morrison's "Rootedness: The Ancestor in Afro-American Fiction," in *Black Women Writers (1950–1980): A Critical Evaluation*, edited by Mari Evans (Garden City, NY: Anchor Press, 1984), pp. 343–378. And see Farah Jasmine Griffin's excellent *"Who Set You Flowin'?": The African-American Migration Narrative* (New York: Oxford University Press, 1995). Griffin does not mention Douglass and the root, but her discussion of ancestors and "safe places" directly informs this discussion.

The power of Sandy's root is tested that Sunday morning when Douglass takes his friend's advice and heads straight back to Covey's place. He immediately sees Covey, who speaks kindly, gives Douglass a minor task, and continues on his way to church. Perhaps the root was working! That Monday morning, the root's efficacy is fully tested. Covey comes at Douglass with a long rope, and sets about tying him up for a thrashing. As soon as Douglass realizes Covey's plan, the young man springs away but is again secured. "But at this moment—from whence came the spirit I don't know—I resolved to fight; . . . I seized Covey hard by the throat; and as I did so, I rose. He held on to me, and I to him" (p. 68). They fought for nearly two hours, remembers Douglass. "I considered him as getting entirely the worst end of the bargain; for he had drawn no blood from me, but I had from him. . . . This battle with Covey," says Douglass, "was the *turning-point* in my career as a slave" [emphasis mine]. As a result of the fight, "my long-crushed spirit rose, cowardice departed, bold defiance took its place; and I now resolved that, however long I might remain a slave in form, the day had passed forever when I could be a slave in fact. I did not hesitate to let it be known of me, that the white man who expected to succeed in whipping, must also succeed in killing me." Covey never touches him again, and in the four remaining years of his bondage, "I had several fights, but was never whipped" (p. 69).

The fight with Covey indicates that to survive slavery Douglass needs the strategies of both trickster and strongman—"the hare and the bear," as Ralph Ellison once put it. Still the presence of the good-luck root (rabbit's-foot–like charm that it is) makes clear that stealth and other qualities represented by the root are more important than sheer physical force in reversing Douglass's fortunes. Chiasmus—the art of turning things around—was working as a hard-bought strategy in Douglass's life before he had learned to master it as a figure of speech.

Silence and masquerade are also key ingredients in Douglass's reversal of fortune. It is a commonplace of Douglass criticism to underscore the writer's refusal to let his reader know exactly how he got away, lest future runaways lose an effective avenue of escape. In this same spirit, Douglass refrains from thanking the poor white boys on the streets of Baltimore who, when he was a young boy, traded

Douglass's bread for reading lessons, "that more valuable bread of knowledge. I am strongly tempted to give the names of two or three of those little boys, as a testimonial of the gratitude and affection I bear them; but prudence forbids;—not that it would injure me, but it might embarrass them; for it is almost an unpardonable offence to teach slaves to read in this Christian country." He reveals only the street name on which they lived and indicates that they not only taught a slave to read but also were troubled when they learned his legal status. "They would express for me the liveliest sympathy, and console me with the hope that something would occur by which I might be free" (p. 44).

These particular instances of purposive silence in fact lend credibility to the entire *Narrative*, and there are several other important scenes in which silence speaks more clearly than words. At times, for instance, Douglass does not describe a scene that he finds too complexly moving to convey in words. Such is the case when Aunt Hester is beaten as he looks on in horror. This entrance to slavery's bloody gate "was a most terrible spectacle," he says. "I wish I could commit to paper the feelings with which I beheld it" (p. 20).

Elsewhere, silence is a strategy for the slave's survival in the tricksters' world. Colonel Lloyd owned so many slaves

> that he did not know them when he saw them; nor did all the slaves of the out-farms know him. It is reported of him, that, while riding along the road one day, he met a colored man, and addressed him in the usual manner of speaking to colored people on the public highways of the south: "Well, boy, whom do you belong to?" "To Colonel Lloyd," replied the slave. "Well, does the colonel treat you well?" "No, sir," was the ready reply. "What, does he work you too hard?" "Yes, sir." "Well, don't he give you enough to eat?" "Yes, sir, he gives me enough, such as it is." (p. 30).

A few weeks later the poor man, who never realized he had been speaking to Colonel Lloyd himself, is sold to a Georgia trader as punishment for finding fault with his master. "This is the penalty of telling the truth, of telling the simple truth, in answer to a series of plain questions." Sometimes spies were sent among the slaves to report their views to their master. This constant danger, says Douglass,

explains why slaves routinely assured whites that they were contented, and established among the slaves the saying, "a still tongue
makes a wise head" (p. 30). Perhaps it is with these words in mind
that Douglass passes the word among his fellow escapees, once they
are betrayed: *"Own nothing,"* he says, (meaning "admit nothing") "and
'Own nothing!' said we all" (p. 81).

These strategies of silence and masquerade come into play in the
final days of Douglass's career as a slave. Here, too, the maxim that
geography is fate proved true. Each move—from the remote farm to
the Great House Farm, and from the Great House Farm to Baltimore, and even the trip back to eastern Maryland where he faced
Covey—proved to be progressive steps. Clearly, the more complex
and variegated the setting, the easier it would be to get away. In a
large port town like Baltimore, so many people from so many back-
grounds came and went that the trickster-trained slave could turn
many situations to his or her advantage or, given a piece of luck,
could simply vanish.

Working as a caulker in Baltimore, Douglass earned from six to
nine dollars a week, and he turned it all over to Master Hugh. To encourage him to keep up the good work, Hugh would sometimes give
Douglass six cents. This gift had the opposite effect, admits Douglass. "I regarded it as a sort of admission of my right to the whole"
(p. 89). Eventually, at his own suggestion, Douglass begins to hire out
his time; but only with the understanding that he must cover all his
own expenses and bring the master his money come rain or come
shine. Because it afforded greater independence, Douglass agrees to
this arrangement; but his analysis of it shows that he was not being
fooled: The deal "was decidedly in my master's favor," writes Douglass. "It relieved him of all need of looking after me. His money was
sure." Fascinatingly, Douglass frames part of his analysis in terms
close to those of a chiasmus. Of the master, Douglass says: "He received all the benefits of slaveholding without its evils; while I endured all the evils of a slave, and suffered all the care and anxiety of
a freeman" (p. 90).

But it is Douglass who will force the final reversal of terms. Re-
solving to run away, he acts as if he has taken to heart Hugh's advice,
which was "to content myself, and be obedient, . . . lay out no plans
to the future" (p. 90). To put Hugh's mind at rest, Douglass brings

him more money than originally contracted. "He seemed very well pleased. . . . He little knew what my plans were. My object in working steadily was to remove any suspicion he might entertain of my intent to run away; and in this I succeeded admirably. I suppose he thought I was never better satisfied with my condition than at the very time during which I was planning my escape." Master Hugh is so pleased by Douglass's faithfulness that he rewards him with twenty-five cents, "quite a large sum for a slaveholder to give a slave," observes Douglass, "and bade me to make a good use of it. I told him I would" (p. 92).

On September 3, 1838, Douglass escaped to New York. "How I did so,—what means I adopted,—what direction I travelled, and by what mode of conveyance,—I must leave unexplained, for the reasons before mentioned" (pp. 92–93). He is off toward taking his place in the abolition movement. Here, indeed, is another key instance of chiasmus, as the man who has learned to keep silent and "own nothing" prepares to take his place as a speaker and writer whose words will not go away.

Finding himself in a thick briar patch with tricksters owning power that is nearly absolute, Douglass quickly learns to become something of a trickster himself. Finding himself ruled by a system of what he terms Lynch Law—the arbitrary prerogatives of those who have all the official power—Douglass learns to read and write; in so doing he develops a rhetorical strategy that trains his mind for revolutionary action, for literally turning the tables on the powerful. He learns to write sentences that outlast theirs; and then, through speeches and through his speechlike narrative, he helps generation after generation of those seeking freedom to find their way from learning how a man or woman becomes a slave to knowing how a slave becomes a man or woman.

This vital knowledge, and the images of freedom through conscientious struggle, ultimately served me well as equipment for living, helping me to survive both the Boston and the Harvard of those difficult years. Perhaps eventually it helped my Boston student as well. I hope that as she made her own leap toward the sense of possibility embodied in the high school diploma and college degree, she made another leap as well: toward recognizing Douglass not as her adversary but as her own great-great-grandfather—for in art there are no degrees of separation—and an inspiration to her own daughters and sons and granddaughters- and grandsons-to-be. I truly hope she came to know that Douglass was working those roots for reversals of ill fortune not just for himself or for me and my people, but for us all.

Robert G. O'Meally is Zora Neale Hurston Professor of Literature at Columbia University, where he has served on the faculty for thirteen years; since 1999 he has been the Director of Columbia's Center for Jazz Studies. He is the author of *The Craft of Ralph Ellison* (1980) and *Lady Day: The Many Faces of Billie Holiday* (1991), and the principal writer of *Seeing Jazz* (1997), the catalog for the Smithsonian Institution's exhibit on jazz painting and literature. He edited the collection of essays *Living with Music: Ralph Ellison's Jazz Writings* (2001) and *The Jazz Cadence of American Culture* (1998), which was awarded a 1999 ASCAP–Deems Taylor award, and coedited *History and Memory in African-American Culture* (1994) and *The Norton Anthology of African American Literature* (1996). O'Meally wrote the script for the documentary film *Lady Day* and for the documentary accompanying the Smithsonian exhibit *Duke Ellington: Beyond Category* (1995); he was nominated for a Grammy for his work as coproducer of the five-CD boxed set *The Jazz Singers* (1998). He lives in New York with his wife, Jacqui Malone, and their sons, Douglass and Gabriel.

NARRATIVE OF THE LIFE OF FREDERICK DOUGLASS, AN AMERICAN SLAVE

PREFACE*

IN THE MONTH OF August, 1841, I attended an anti-slavery convention in Nantucket, at which it was my happiness to become acquainted with FREDERICK DOUGLASS, the writer of the following
Narrative. He was a stranger to nearly every member of that body;
but, having recently made his escape from the southern prison-house
of bondage,[1] and feeling his curiosity excited to ascertain the principles and measures of the abolitionists,—of whom he had heard a
somewhat vague description while he was a slave,—he was induced
to give his attendance, on the occasion alluded to, though at that time
a resident in New Bedford.

Fortunate, most fortunate occurrence!—fortunate for the millions of
his manacled brethren, yet panting for deliverance from their awful
thraldom!—fortunate for the cause of negro emanicpation, and of universal liberty!—fortunate for the land of his birth, which he has already
done so much to save and bless!—fortunate for a large circle of friends
and acquaintances, whose sympathy and affection he has strongly secured by the many sufferings he has endured, by his virtuous traits of
character, by his ever abiding remembrance of those who are in bonds,
as being bound with them!—fortunate for the multitudes, in various
parts of our republic, whose minds he has enlightened on the subject of
slavery, and who have been melted to tears by his pathos, or roused to
virtuous indignation by his stirring eloquence against the enslavers of
men!—fortunate for himself, as it at once brought him into the field of
public usefulness, "gave the world assurance of a MAN,"[2] quickened the
slumbering energies of his soul, and consecrated him to the great work
of breaking the rod of the oppressor, and letting the oppressed go free!

I shall never forget his first speech at the convention[3]—the extraordinary emotion it excited in my own mind—the powerful impression it created upon a crowded auditory,† completely taken by

---

*The author of the preface is William Lloyd Garrison (1805–1879), a well-known
abolitionist. Garrison was a founder of the American Anti-Slavery Society in 1833 as
well as the founder and publisher of *The Liberator*, the well-known antislavery newspaper published from 1831 to 1865.
†Auditorium.

surprise—the applause which followed from the beginning to the end of his felicitous remarks. I think I never hated slavery so intensely as at that moment; certainly, my perception of the enormous outrage which is inflicted by it, on the godlike nature of its victims, was rendered far more clear than ever. There stood one, in physical proportion and stature commanding and exact—in intellect richly endowed—in natural eloquence a prodigy—in soul manifestly "created but a little lower than the angels"*—yet a slave, ay, a fugitive slave,—trembling for his safety, hardly daring to believe that on the American soil, a single white person could be found who would befriend him at all hazards, for the love of God and humanity! Capable of high attainments as an intellectual and moral being—needing nothing but a comparatively small amount of cultivation to make him an ornament to society and a blessing to his race—by the law of the land, by the voice of the people, by the terms of the slave code,[4] he was only a piece of property, a beast of burden, a chattel personal,† nevertheless!

A beloved friend from New Bedford[5] prevailed on Mr. DOUGLASS to address the convention. He came forward to the platform with a hesitancy and embarrassment, necessarily the attendants of a sensitive mind in such a novel position. After apologizing for his ignorance, and reminding the audience that slavery was a poor school for the human intellect and heart, he proceeded to narrate some of the facts in his own history as a slave, and in the course of his speech gave utterance to many noble thoughts and thrilling reflections. As soon as he had taken his seat, filled with hope and admiration, I rose, and declared that PATRICK HENRY, of revolutionary fame,[6] never made a speech more eloquent in the cause of liberty, than the one we had just listened to from the lips of that hunted fugitive. So I believed at that time—such is my belief now. I reminded the audience of the peril which surrounded this self-emancipated young man at the North,—even in Massachusetts, on the soil of the Pilgrim Fathers, among the descendants of revolutionary sires; and I appealed to them, whether they would ever allow him to be carried back into slavery,—law or no

---

*Reference to the Bible (Psalms 8:5 and Hebrews 2:7–9).
†Legal term for movable personal property, such as a horse.

law, constitution or no constitution. The response was unanimous and in thunder-tones—"NO!" "Will you succor and protect him as a brother-man—a resident of the old Bay State?"* "YES!" shouted the whole mass, with an energy so startling, that the ruthless tyrants south of Mason and Dixon's line† might almost have heard the mighty burst of feeling, and recognized it as the pledge of an invincible determination, on the part of those who gave it, never to betray him that wanders, but to hide the outcast, and firmly to abide the consequences.

It was at once deeply impressed upon my mind, that, if Mr. DOUGLASS could be persuaded to consecrate his time and talents to the promotion of the anti-slavery enterprise, a powerful impetus would be given to it, and a stunning blow at the same time inflicted on northern prejudice against a colored complexion. I therefore endeavored to instill hope and courage into his mind, in order that he might dare to engage in a vocation so anomalous and responsible for a person in his situation; and I was seconded in this effort by warm-hearted friends, especially by the late General Agent of the Massachusetts Anti-Slavery Society, Mr. JOHN A. COLLINS,[7] whose judgment in this instance entirely coincided with my own. At first, he could give no encouragement; with unfeigned diffidence,‡ he expressed his conviction that he was not adequate to the performance of so great a task; the path marked out was wholly an untrodden one; he was sincerely apprehensive that he should do more harm than good. After much deliberation, however, he consented to make a trial; and ever since that period, he has acted as a lecturing agent, under the auspices either of the American or the Massachusetts Anti-Slavery Society. In labors he has been most abundant; and his success in combating prejudice, in gaining proselytes,§ in agitating the public mind, has far surpassed the most sanguine expectations that were raised at the commencement of his brilliant career. He has borne himself with gentleness and meekness, yet with true manliness

---

*Massachusetts.
†Boundary between Maryland and Pennsylvania; symbolic dividing line between the slave South and the free North before the Civil War.
‡Frank uncertainty.
§Converts.

of character. As a public speaker, he excels in pathos, wit, compari-
son, imitation, strength of reasoning, and fluency of language. There
is in him that union of head and heart, which is indispensable to an
enlightenment of the heads and a winning of the hearts of others.
May his strength continue to be equal to his day! May he continue
to "grow in grace, and in the knowledge of God,"* that he may be increasingly serviceable in the cause of bleeding humanity, whether at
home or abroad!

It is certainly a very remarkable fact, that one of the most efficient
advocates of the slave population, now before the public, is a fugitive
slave, in the person of FREDERICK DOUGLASS; and that the free colored population of the United States are as ably represented by one
of their own number, in the person of CHARLES LENOX REMOND,[8]
whose eloquent appeals have extorted the highest applause of multitudes on both sides of the Atlantic. Let the calumniators† of the colored race despise themselves for their baseness and illiberality of
spirit, and henceforth cease to talk of the natural inferiority of those
who require nothing but time and opportunity to attain to the highest point of human excellence.

It may, perhaps, be fairly questioned, whether any other portion of
the population of the earth could have endured the privations, sufferings and horrors of slavery, without having become more degraded
in the scale of humanity than the slaves of African descent. Nothing
has been left undone to cripple their intellects, darken their minds,
debase their moral nature, obliterate all traces of their relationship to
mankind; and yet how wonderfully they have sustained the mighty
load of a most frightful bondage, under which they have been groan-
ing for centuries! To illustrate the effect of slavery on the white
man,—to show that he has no powers of endurance, in such a condition, superior to those of his black brother,—DANIEL O'CONNELL,[9]
the distinguished advocate of universal emancipation, and the might-
iest champion of prostrate but not conquered Ireland, relates the following anecdote in a speech delivered by him in the Conciliation
Hall, Dublin, before the Loyal National Repeal Association, March

---

*Reference to the Bible, 2 Peter 3:18.
†Maligners; slanderers.

31, 1845. "No matter," said Mr. O'CONNELL, "under what specious term it may disguise itself, slavery is still hideous. *It has a natural, an inevitable tendency to brutalize every noble faculty of man.* An American sailor, who was cast away on the shore of Africa, where he was kept in slavery for three years, was, at the expiration of that period, found to be imbruted and stultified*—he had lost all reasoning power; and having forgotten his native language, could only utter some savage gibberish between Arabic and English, which nobody could understand, and which even he himself found difficulty in pronouncing. So much for the humanizing influence of THE DOMESTIC INSTITUTION!"† Admitting this to have been an extraordinary case of mental deterioration, it proves at least that the white slave can sink as low in the scale of humanity as the black one.

Mr. DOUGLASS has very properly chosen to write his own Narrative, in his own style, and according to the best of his ability, rather than to employ some one else. It is, therefore, entirely his own production; and, considering how long and dark was the career he had to run as a slave,—how few have been his opportunities to improve his mind since he broke his iron fetters,—it is, in my judgment, highly creditable to his head and heart. He who can peruse it without a tearful eye, a heaving breast, an afflicted spirit,—without being filled with an unutterable abhorrence of slavery and all its abettors,‡ and animated with a determination to seek the immediate overthrow of that execrable§ system,—without trembling for the fate of this country in the hands of a righteous God, who is ever on the side of the oppressed, and whose arm is not shortened that it cannot save,— must have a flinty heart, and be qualified to act the part of a trafficker "in slaves and the souls of men."‖ I am confident that it is essentially true in all its statements; that nothing has been set down in malice, nothing exaggerated, nothing drawn from the imagination; that it

---

*Degraded to the state of a beast (imbruted) and rendered useless or ridiculous (stultified).

†Meanng slavery (with its pretensions to domesticity or cultural usefulness).

‡Advocates.

§Detestable.

‖Reference to the Bible, Revelation 18:13.

comes short of the reality, rather than overstates a single fact in regard to SLAVERY AS IT IS.[10] The experience of FREDERICK DOUG-
LASS, as a slave, was not a peculiar one; his lot was not especially a
hard one; his case may be regarded as a very fair specimen of the
treatment of slaves in Maryland, in which State it is conceded that
they are better fed and less cruelly treated than in Georgia, Alabama,
or Louisiana. Many have suffered incomparably more, while very few
on the plantations have suffered less, than himself. Yet how de-
plorable was his situation! what terrible chastisements were inflicted
upon his person! what still more shocking outrages were perpetrated
upon his mind! with all his noble powers and sublime aspirations,
how like a brute was he treated, even by those professing to have the
same mind in them that was in Christ Jesus! to what dreadful liabilities was he continually subjected! how destitute of friendly counsel
and aid, even in his greatest extremities! how heavy was the midnight
of woe which shrouded in blackness the last ray of hope, and filled
the future with terror and gloom! what longings after freedom took
possession of his breast, and how his misery augmented, in proportion as he grew reflective and intelligent,—thus demonstrating that
a happy slave is an extinct man! how he thought, reasoned, felt, under
the lash of the driver, with the chains upon his limbs! what perils he
encountered in his endeavors to escape from his horrible doom! and
how signal have been his deliverance and preservation in the midst of
a nation of pitiless enemies!

This Narrative contains many affecting incidents, many passages
of great eloquence and power; but I think the most thrilling one of
them all is the description DOUGLASS gives of his feelings, as he
stood soliloquizing respecting his fate, and the chances of his one day
being a freeman, on the banks of the Chesapeake Bay—viewing the
receding vessels as they flew with their white wings before the
breeze, and apostrophizing* them as animated by the living spirit of
freedom. Who can read that passage, and be insensible to its pathos
and sublimity? Compressed into it is a whole Alexandrian library† of

---

*Addressing a personified abstraction or an absent or imaginary person in a rhetori-
cal fashion.
†One of the most famous libraries of the Greco-Roman world (third century B.C.),
thought to have contained more than 400,000 books.

thought, feeling, and sentiment—all that can, all that need be urged, in the form of expostulation, entreaty, rebuke, against that crime of crimes,—making man the property of his fellow-man! O, how accursed is that system, which entombs the godlike mind of man, defaces the divine image, reduces those who by creation were crowned with glory and honor to a level with four-footed beasts, and exalts the dealer in human flesh above all that is called God! Why should its existence be prolonged one hour? Is it not evil, only evil, and that continually? What does its presence imply but the absence of all fear of God, all regard for man, on the part of the people of the United States? Heaven speed its eternal overthrow!

So profoundly ignorant of the nature of slavery are many persons, that they are stubbornly incredulous whenever they read or listen to any recital of the cruelties which are daily inflicted on its victims. They do not deny that the slaves are held as property; but that terrible fact seems to convey to their minds no idea of injustice, exposure to outrage, or savage barbarity. Tell them of cruel scourgings, of mutilations and brandings, of scenes of pollution and blood, of the banishment of all light and knowledge, and they affect to be greatly indignant at such enormous exaggerations, such wholesale misstatements, such abominable libels on the character of the southern planters! As if all these direful outrages were not the natural results of slavery! As if it were less cruel to reduce a human being to the condition of a thing, than to give him a severe flagellation, or to deprive him of necessary food and clothing! As if whips, chains, thumbscrews, paddles, bloodhounds, overseers, drivers, patrols, were not all indispensable to keep the slaves down, and to give protection to their ruthless oppressors! As if, when the marriage institution is abolished, concubinage,* adultery, and incest, must not necessarily abound; when all the rights of humanity are annihilated, any barrier remains to protect the victim from the fury of the spoiler; when absolute power is assumed over life and liberty, it will not be wielded with destructive sway! Skeptics of this character abound in society. In some few instances, their incredulity arises from a want of reflection; but, generally, it indicates a hatred of the light, a desire to shield slavery

---

*Cohabitation without legal marriage.

from the assaults of its foes, a contempt of the colored race, whether bond or free. Such will try to discredit the shocking tales of slave-holding cruelty which are recorded in this truthful Narrative; but they will labor in vain. Mr. DOUGLASS has frankly disclosed the place of his birth, the names of those who claimed ownership in his body and soul, and the names also of those who committed the crimes which he has alleged against them. His statements, therefore, may easily be disproved, if they are untrue.

In the course of his Narrative, he relates two instances of murderous cruelty,—in one of which a planter deliberately shot a slave belonging to a neighboring plantation, who had unintentionally gotten within his lordly domain in quest of fish; and in the other, an overseer blew out the brains of a slave who had fled to a stream of water to escape a bloody scourging. Mr. DOUGLASS states that in neither of these instances was any thing done by way of legal arrest or judicial investigation. The Baltimore American, of March 17, 1845, relates a similar case of atrocity, perpetrated with similar impunity—as follows:—"*Shooting a Slave.*—We learn, upon the authority of a letter from Charles county, Maryland, received by a gentleman of this city, that a young man, named Matthews, a nephew of General Matthews, and whose father, it is believed, holds an office at Washington, killed one of the slaves upon his father's farm by shooting him. The letter states that young Matthews had been left in charge of the farm; that he gave an order to the servant, which was disobeyed, when he proceeded to the house, *obtained a gun, and, returning, shot the servant.* He immediately, the letter continues, fled to his father's residence, where he still remains unmolested."—Let it never be forgotten, that no slaveholder or overseer can be convicted of any outrage perpetrated on the person of a slave, however diabolical it may be, on the testimony of colored witnesses, whether bond or free. By the slave code, they are adjudged to be as incompetent to testify against a white man, as though they were indeed a part of the brute creation. Hence, there is no legal protection in fact, whatever there may be in form, for the slave population; and any amount of cruelty may be inflicted on them with impunity. Is it possible for the human mind to conceive of a more horrible state of society?

The effect of a religious profession on the conduct of southern masters is vividly described in the following Narrative, and shown to be any thing but salutary. In the nature of the case, it must be in the highest degree pernicious. The testimony of Mr. DOUGLASS, on this point, is sustained by a cloud of witnesses, whose veracity is unimpeachable.* "A slaveholder's profession of Christianity is a palpable imposture. He is a felon of the highest grade. He is a man-stealer. It is of no importance what you put in the other scale."

Reader! are you with the man-stealers in sympathy and purpose, or on the side of their down-trodden victims? If with the former, then are you the foe of God and man. If with the latter, what are you prepared to do and dare in their behalf? Be faithful, be vigilant, be untiring in your efforts to break every yoke, and let the oppressed go free. Come what may—cost what it may—inscribe on the banner which you unfurl to the breeze, as your religious and political motto—"NO COMPROMISE WITH SLAVERY! NO UNION WITH SLAVEHOLDERS!"[11]

Wm. Lloyd Garrison
Boston, May 1, 1845.

---

*Without doubt.

LETTER FROM
WENDELL PHILLIPS, ESQ.*

Boston, *April* 22, 1845.

My Dear Friend:

You remember the old fable of "The Man and the Lion," where the lion complained that he should not be so misrepresented "when the lions wrote history."

I am glad the time has come when the "lions write history." We have been left long enough to gather the character of slavery from the involuntary evidence of the masters. One might, indeed, rest sufficiently satisfied with what, it is evident, must be, in general, the results of such a relation, without seeking further to find whether they have followed in every instance. Indeed, those who stare at the half-peck of corn a week, and love to count the lashes on the slave's back, are seldom the "stuff" out of which reformers and abolitionists are to be made. I remember that, in 1838, many were waiting for the results of the West India experiment,[12] before they could come into our ranks. Those "results" have come long ago; but, alas! few of that number have come with them, as converts. A man must be disposed to judge of emancipation by other tests than whether it has increased the produce of sugar,—and to hate slavery for other reasons than because it starves men and whips women,—before he is ready to lay the first stone of his anti-slavery life.

I was glad to learn, in your story, how early the most neglected of God's children waken to a sense of their rights, and of the injustice done them. Experience is a keen teacher; and long before you had mastered your A B C, or knew where the "white sails" of the Chesapeake were bound, you began, I see, to gauge the wretchedness of the slave, not by his hunger and want, not by his lashes and toil, but by the cruel and blighting death which gathers over his soul.

In connection with this, there is one circumstance which makes

*A Harvard-trained attorney and leading abolitionist orator (1811–1884), he was a close friend of Douglass through the 1840s and served as president of the Anti-Slavery Society from 1865 to 1870.

your recollections peculiarly valuable, and renders your early insight the more remarkable. You come from that part of the country where we are told slavery appears with its fairest features. Let us hear, then, what it is at its best estate—gaze on its bright side, if it has one; and then imagination may task her powers to add dark lines to the picture, as she travels southward to that (for the colored man) Valley of the Shadow of Death, where the Mississippi sweeps along.

Again, we have known you long, and can put the most entire confidence in your truth, candor, and sincerity. Every one who has heard you speak has felt, and, I am confident, every one who reads your book will feel, persuaded that you give them a fair specimen of the whole truth. No one-sided portrait,—no wholesale complaints,—but strict justice done, whenever individual kindliness has neutralized, for a moment, the deadly system with which it was strangely allied. You have been with us, too, some years, and can fairly compare the twilight of rights, which your race enjoy at the North, with that "noon of night" under which they labor south of Mason and Dixon's line. Tell us whether, after all, the half-free colored man of Massachusetts is worse off than the pampered slave of the rice swamps!

In reading your life, no one can say that we have unfairly picked out some rare specimens of cruelty. We know that the bitter drops, which even you have drained from the cup, are no incidental aggravations, no individual ills, but such as must mingle always and necessarily in the lot of every slave. They are the essential ingredients, not the occasional results, of the system.

After all, I shall read your book with trembling for you. Some years ago, when you were beginning to tell me your real name and birthplace, you may remember I stopped you, and preferred to remain ignorant of all. With the exception of a vague description, so I continued, till the other day, when you read me your memoirs. I hardly knew, at the time, whether to thank you or not for the sight of them, when I reflected that it was still dangerous, in Massachusetts, for honest men to tell their names! They say the fathers, in 1776, signed the Declaration of Independence with the halter* about their necks. You, too, publish your declaration of freedom with danger compassing† you around.

---

*Rope or strap for leading animals.
†Encircling.

In all the broad lands which the Constitution of the United States overshadows, there is no single spot,—however narrow or desolate,—where a fugitive slave can plant himself and say, "I am safe." The whole armory of Northern Law has no shield for you. I am free to say that, in your place, I should throw the MS. into the fire.

You, perhaps, may tell your story in safety, endeared as you are to so many warm hearts by rare gifts, and a still rarer devotion of them to the service of others. But it will be owing only to your labors, and the fearless efforts of those who, trampling the laws and Constitution of the country under their feet, are determined that they will "hide the outcast," and that their hearths shall be, spite of the law, an asylum for the oppressed, if, some time or other, the humblest may stand in our streets, and bear witness in safety against the cruelties of which he has been the victim.

Yet it is sad to think, that these very throbbing hearts which welcome your story, and form your best safeguard in telling it, are all beating contrary to the "statute in such case made and provided." Go on, my dear friend, till you, and those who, like you, have been saved, so as by fire, from the dark prison-house, shall stereotype* these free, illegal pulses into statutes; and New England, cutting loose from a blood-stained Union, shall glory in being the house of refuge for the oppressed;—till we no longer merely "*hide* the outcast,"† or make a merit of standing idly by while he is hunted in our midst; but, consecrating anew the soil of the Pilgrims as an asylum for the oppressed, proclaim our *welcome* to the slave so loudly, that the tones shall reach every hut in the Carolinas, and make the broken-hearted bondman leap up at the thought of old Massachusetts.

God speed the day!

Till then, and ever,

Yours truly,

Wendell Phillips

---

*The verb is used here in a positive sense, meaning "print or perpetuate in unchanging form."
†Reference to the Bible, Isaiah 16:3.

CHAPTER I

I WAS BORN IN Tuckahoe, near Hillsborough, and about twelve miles from Easton, in Talbot county, Maryland. I have no accurate knowledge of my age, never having seen any authentic record containing it.[13] By far the larger part of the slaves know as little of their ages as horses know of theirs, and it is the wish of most masters within my knowledge to keep their slaves thus ignorant. I do not remember to have ever met a slave who could tell of his birthday. They seldom come nearer to it than planting-time, harvest-time, cherry-time, spring-time, or fall-time. A want of information concerning my own was a source of unhappiness to me even during childhood. The white children could tell their ages. I could not tell why I ought to be deprived of the same privilege. I was not allowed to make any inquiries of my master concerning it. He deemed all such inquiries on the part of a slave improper and impertinent, and evidence of a restless spirit. The nearest estimate I can give makes me now between twenty-seven and twenty-eight years of age. I come to this, from hearing my master say, some time during 1835, I was about seventeen years old.

My mother was named Harriet Bailey. She was the daughter of Isaac and Betsey Bailey, both colored, and quite dark. My mother was of a darker complexion than either my grandmother or grandfather.

My father was a white man.[14] He was admitted to be such by all I ever heard speak of my parentage. The opinion was also whispered that my master was my father; but of the correctness of this opinion, I know nothing; the means of knowing was withheld from me. My mother and I were separated when I was but an infant—before I knew her as my mother. It is a common custom, in the part of Maryland from which I ran away, to part children from their mothers at a very early age. Frequently, before the child has reached its twelfth month, its mother is taken from it, and hired out on some farm a considerable distance off, and the child is placed under the care of an old woman, too old for field labor. For what this separation is done, I do not know, unless it be to hinder the development of the

child's affection toward its mother, and to blunt and destroy the natural affection of the mother for the child. This is the inevitable result.

I never saw my mother, to know her as such, more than four or
five times in my life; and each of those times was very short in dura-
tion, and at night. She was hired by a Mr. Stewart, who lived about
twelve miles from my home. She made her journeys to see me in the
night, travelling the whole distance on foot, after the performance of
her day's work. She was a field hand, and a whipping is the penalty
of not being in the field at sunrise, unless a slave has special permission from his or her master to the contrary—a permission which they
seldom get, and one that gives to him that gives it the proud name of
being a kind master. I do not recollect of ever seeing my mother by
the light of day. She was with me in the night. She would lie down
with me, and get me to sleep, but long before I waked she was gone.
Very little communication ever took place between us. Death soon
ended what little we could have while she lived, and with it her hardships and suffering. She died when I was about seven years old, on
one of my master's farms, near Lee's Mill. I was not allowed to be
present during her illness, at her death, or burial. She was gone long
before I knew any thing about it. Never having enjoyed, to any considerable extent, her soothing presence, her tender and watchful care,
I received the tidings of her death with much the same emotions I
should have probably felt at the death of a stranger.

Called thus suddenly away, she left me without the slightest inti-
mation of who my father was. The whisper that my master was my
father, may or may not be true; and, true or false, it is of but little consequence to my purpose whilst the fact remains, in all its glaring odi-
ousness, that slaveholders have ordained, and by law established, that
the children of slave women shall in all cases follow the condition of
their mothers; and this is done too obviously to administer to their
own lusts, and make a gratification of their wicked desires profitable
as well as pleasurable; for by this cunning arrangement, the slaveholder, in cases not a few, sustains to his slaves the double relation of
master and father.

I know of such cases; and it is worthy of remark that such slaves
invariably suffer greater hardships, and have more to contend with,
than others. They are, in the first place, a constant offence to their

mistress. She is ever disposed to find fault with them; they can seldom do any thing to please her; she is never better pleased than when
she sees them under the lash, especially when she suspects her husband of showing to his mulatto children favors which he withholds
from his black slaves. The master is frequently compelled to sell this
class of his slaves, out of deference to the feelings of his white wife;
and, cruel as the deed may strike any one to be, for a man to sell his
own children to human flesh-mongers, it is often the dictate of humanity for him to do so; for, unless he does this, he must not only
whip them himself, but must stand by and see one white son tie up
his brother, of but few shades darker complexion than himself, and
ply the gory lash to his naked back; and if he lisp one word of disap-
proval, it is set down to his parental partiality, and only makes a bad
matter worse, both for himself and the slave whom he would protect
and defend.

Every year brings with it multitudes of this class of slaves. It was
doubtless in consequence of a knowledge of this fact, that one great
statesman of the south predicted the downfall of slavery by the inevitable laws of population. Whether this prophecy is ever fulfilled or
not, it is nevertheless plain that a very different-looking class of people are springing up at the south, and are now held in slavery, from
those originally brought to this country from Africa; and if their increase will do no other good, it will do away the force of the argument, that God cursed Ham,[15] and therefore American slavery is
right. If the lineal descendants of Ham are alone to be scripturally
enslaved, it is certain that slavery at the south must soon become un-
scriptural; for thousands are ushered into the world, annually, who,
like myself, owe their existence to white fathers, and those fathers
most frequently their own masters.

I have had two masters. My first master's name was Anthony. I do
not remember his first name. He was generally called Captain Anthony—a title which, I presume, he acquired by sailing a craft on the
Chesapeake Bay. He was not considered a rich slaveholder. He
owned two or three farms, and about thirty slaves. His farms and
slaves were under the care of an overseer. The overseer's name was
Plummer. Mr. Plummer was a miserable drunkard, a profane swearer,
and a savage monster. He always went armed with a cowskin and a
heavy cudgel.* I have known him to cut and slash the women's heads

so horribly, that even master would be enraged at his cruelty, and
would threaten to whip him if he did not mind himself. Master, however, was not a humane slaveholder. It required extraordinary barbarity on the part of an overseer to affect him. He was a cruel man,
hardened by a long life of slaveholding. He would at times seem to
take great pleasure in whipping a slave. I have often been awakened
at the dawn of day by the most heartrending shrieks of an own aunt
of mine, whom he used to tie up to a joist, and whip upon her naked
back till she was literally covered with blood. No words, no tears, no
prayers, from his gory victim, seemed to move his iron heart from its
bloody purpose. The louder she screamed, the harder he whipped;
and where the blood ran fastest, there he whipped longest. He would
whip her to make her scream, and whip her to make her hush; and
not until overcome by fatigue, would he cease to swing the blood-
clotted cowskin. I remember the first time I ever witnessed this horrible exhibition. I was quite a child, but I well remember it. I never
shall forget it whilst I remember any thing. It was the first of a long
series of such outrages, of which I was doomed to be a witness and a
participant. It struck me with awful force. It was the blood-stained
gate, the entrance to the hell of slavery, through which I was about
to pass. It was a most terrible spectacle. I wish I could commit to
paper the feelings with which I beheld it.

This occurrence took place very soon after I went to live with my
old master, and under the following circumstances. Aunt Hester
went out one night,—where or for what I do not know,—and happened to be absent when my master desired her presence. He had ordered her not to go out evenings, and warned her that she must never
let him catch her in company with a young man, who was paying attention to her belonging to Colonel Lloyd.[16] The young man's name
was Ned Roberts, generally called Lloyd's Ned. Why master was so
careful of her, may be safely left to conjecture. She was a woman of
noble form, and of graceful proportions, having very few equals, and
fewer superiors, in personal appearance, among the colored or white
women of our neighborhood.

Aunt Hester had not only disobeyed his orders in going out, but
had been found in company with Lloyd's Ned; which circumstance,

---

*A cowskin is a whip made of raw cowhide; a cudgel is a short, heavy club.

I found, from what he said while whipping her, was the chief offence. Had he been a man of pure morals himself, he might have been thought interested in protecting the innocence of my aunt; but those who knew him will not suspect him of any such virtue. Before he commenced whipping Aunt Hester, he took her into the kitchen, and stripped her from neck to waist, leaving her neck, shoulders, and back, entirely naked. He then told her to cross her hands, calling her at the same time a d——d b——h. After crossing her hands, he tied them with a strong rope, and led her to a stool under a large hook in the joist,* put in for the purpose. He made her get upon the stool, and tied her hands to the hook. She now stood fair for his infernal purpose. Her arms were stretched up at their full length, so that she stood upon the ends of her toes. He then said to her, "Now, you d——d b——h, I'll learn you how to disobey my orders!" and after rolling up his sleeves, he commenced to lay on the heavy cowskin, and soon the warm, red blood (amid heartrending shrieks from her, and horrid oaths from him) came dripping to the floor. I was so terrified and horror-stricken at the sight, that I hid myself in a closet, and dared not venture out till long after the bloody transaction was over. I expected it would be my turn next. It was all new to me. I had never seen any thing like it before. I had always lived with my grandmother on the outskirts of the plantation, where she was put to raise the children of the younger women. I had therefore been, until now, out of the way of the bloody scenes that often occurred on the plantation.

---

*One of the timbers on which the boards of a floor or ceiling are nailed.

CHAPTER II

MY MASTER'S FAMILY CONSISTED of two sons, Andrew and Richard; one daughter, Lucretia, and her husband, Captain Thomas Auld. They lived in one house, upon the home plantation of Colonel Edward Lloyd. My master was Colonel Lloyd's clerk and superintendent. He was what might be called the overseer of the overseers. I spent two years of childhood on this plantation in my old master's family. It was here that I witnessed the bloody transaction recorded in the first chapter; and as I received my first impressions of slavery on this plantation, I will give some description of it, and of slavery as it there existed. The plantation is about twelve miles north of Easton, in Talbot county, and is situated on the border of Miles River. The principal products raised upon it were tobacco, corn, and wheat. These were raised in great abundance; so that, with the products of this and the other farms belonging to him, he was able to keep in almost constant employment a large sloop,* in carrying them to market at Baltimore. This sloop was named Sally Lloyd, in honor of one of the colonel's daughters. My master's son-in-law, Captain Auld, was master of the vessel; she was otherwise manned by the colonel's own slaves. Their names were Peter, Isaac, Rich, and Jake. These were esteemed very highly by the other slaves, and looked upon as the privileged ones of the plantation; for it was no small affair, in the eyes of the slaves, to be allowed to see Baltimore.

Colonel Lloyd kept from three to four hundred slaves on his home plantation, and owned a large number more on the neighboring farms belonging to him. The names of the farms nearest to the home plantation were Wye Town and New Design. "Wye Town" was under the overseership of a man named Noah Willis. New Design was under the overseership of a Mr. Townsend. The overseers of these, and all the rest of the farms, numbering over twenty, received advice and direction from the managers of the home plantation. This was

---

*Single-masted sailing vessel.

the great business place. It was the seat of government for the whole twenty farms. All disputes among the overseers were settled here. If a slave was convicted of any high misdemeanor, became unmanageable, or evinced a determination to run away, he was brought immediately here, severely whipped, put on board the sloop, carried to Baltimore, and sold to Austin Woolfolk, or some other slave-trader,[17] as a warning to the slaves remaining.

Here, too, the slaves of all the other farms received their monthly allowance of food, and their yearly clothing. The men and women slaves received, as their monthly allowance of food, eight pounds of pork, or its equivalent in fish, and one bushel of corn meal. Their yearly clothing consisted of two coarse linen shirts, one pair of linen trousers, like the shirts, one jacket, one pair of trousers for winter, made of coarse negro cloth,* one pair of stockings, and one pair of shoes; the whole of which could not have cost more than seven dollars. The allowance of the slave children was given to their mothers, or the old women having the care of them. The children unable to work in the field had neither shoes, stockings, jackets, nor trousers, given to them; their clothing consisted of two coarse linen shirts per year. When these failed them, they went naked until the next allowance-day. Children from seven to ten years old, of both sexes, almost naked, might be seen at all seasons of the year.

There were no beds given the slaves, unless one coarse blanket be considered such, and none but the men and women had these. This, however, is not considered a very great privation. They find less difficulty from the want of beds, than from the want of time to sleep; for when their day's work in the field is done, the most of them having their washing, mending, and cooking to do, and having few or none of the ordinary facilities for doing either of these, very many of their sleeping hours are consumed in preparing for the field the coming day; and when this is done, old and young, male and female, married and single, drop down side by side, on one common bed,—the cold, damp floor,—each covering himself or herself with their miserable blankets; and here they sleep till they are summoned to the field by the driver's horn. At the sound of this, all must rise, and be off to

---

*Cheap cotton fabric, so named because it was designed to be worn by black subservients.

the field. There must be no halting; every one must be at his or her post; and woe betides them who hear not this morning summons to the field; for if they are not awakened by the sense of hearing, they are by the sense of feeling: no age nor sex finds any favor. Mr. Severe, the overseer, used to stand by the door of the quarter, armed with a large hickory stick and heavy cowskin, ready to whip any one who was so unfortunate as not to hear, or, from any other cause, was prevented from being ready to start for the field at the sound of the horn.

Mr. Severe was rightly named:[18] he was a cruel man. I have seen him whip a woman, causing the blood to run half an hour at the time; and this, too, in the midst of her crying children, pleading for their mother's release. He seemed to take pleasure in manifesting his fiendish barbarity. Added to his cruelty, he was a profane swearer. It was enough to chill the blood and stiffen the hair of an ordinary man to hear him talk. Scarce a sentence escaped him but that was commenced or concluded by some horrid oath. The field was the place to witness his cruelty and profanity. His presence made it both the field of blood and of blasphemy. From the rising till the going down of the sun, he was cursing, raving, cutting, and slashing among the slaves of the field, in the most frightful manner. His career was short. He died very soon after I went to Colonel Lloyd's; and he died as he lived, uttering, with his dying groans, bitter curses and horrid oaths. His death was regarded by the slaves as the result of a merciful Providence.

Mr. Severe's place was filled by a Mr. Hopkins. He was a very different man. He was less cruel, less profane, and made less noise, than Mr. Severe. His course was characterized by no extraordinary demonstrations of cruelty. He whipped, but seemed to take no pleasure in it. He was called by the slaves a good overseer.

The home plantation of Colonel Lloyd wore the appearance of a country village. All the mechanical operations for all the farms were performed here. The shoemaking and mending, the blacksmithing, cartwrighting, coopering,* weaving, and grain-grinding, were all performed by the slaves on the home plantation. The whole place wore

---

*Cartwrighting is the building or repairing of carts; coopering is the making or repairing of wooden tubs or barrels.

a business-like aspect very unlike the neighboring farms. The number of houses, too, conspired to give it advantage over the neighboring farms. It was called by the slaves the *Great House Farm.* Few privileges were esteemed higher, by the slaves of the out-farms, than that of being selected to do errands at the Great House Farm. It was associated in their minds with greatness. A representative could not be prouder of his election to a seat in the American Congress, than a slave on one of the out-farms would be of his election to do errands at the Great House Farm. They regarded it as evidence of great confidence reposed in them by their overseers; and it was on this account, as well as a constant desire to be out of the field from under the driver's lash, that they esteemed it a high privilege, one worth careful living for. He was called the smartest and most trusty fellow, who had this honor conferred upon him the most frequently. The competitors for this office sought as diligently to please their overseers, as the office-seekers in the political parties seek to please and deceive the people. The same traits of character might be seen in Colonel Lloyd's slaves, as are seen in the slaves of the political parties.

The slaves selected to go to the Great House Farm, for the monthly allowance for themselves and their fellow-slaves, were peculiarly enthusiastic. While on their way, they would make the dense old woods, for miles around, reverberate with their wild songs, revealing at once the highest joy and the deepest sadness. They would compose and sing as they went along, consulting neither time nor tune. The thought that came up, came out—if not in the word, in the sound;—and as frequently in the one as in the other. They would sometimes sing the most pathetic sentiment in the most rapturous tone, and the most rapturous sentiment in the most pathetic tone. Into all of their songs they would manage to weave something of the Great House Farm. Especially would they do this, when leaving home. They would then sing most exultingly the following words:—

I am going away to the Great House Farm!
O, yea! O, yea! O!

This they would sing, as a chorus, to words which to many would seem unmeaning jargon, but which, nevertheless, were full of mean-

ing to themselves. I have sometimes thought that the mere hearing
of those songs would do more to impress some minds with the horrible character of slavery, than the reading of whole volumes of philosophy on the subject could do.

I did not, when a slave, understand the deep meaning of those
rude and apparently incoherent songs. I was myself within the circle;
so that I neither saw nor heard as those without might see and hear.
They told a tale of woe which was then altogether beyond my feeble
comprehension; they were tones loud, long, and deep; they breathed
the prayer and complaint of souls boiling over with the bitterest anguish. Every tone was a testimony against slavery, and a prayer to
God for deliverance from chains. The hearing of those wild notes always depressed my spirit, and filled me with ineffable sadness. I have
frequently found myself in tears while hearing them. The mere recurrence to those songs, even now, afflicts me; and while I am writing these lines, an expression of feeling has already found its way
down my cheek. To those songs I trace my first glimmering conception of the dehumanizing character of slavery. I can never get rid of
that conception. Those songs still follow me, to deepen my hatred of
slavery, and quicken my sympathies for my brethren in bonds. If any
one wishes to be impressed with the soul-killing effects of slavery, let
him go to Colonel Lloyd's plantation, and, on allowance-day, place
himself in the deep pine woods, and there let him, in silence, analyze
the sounds that shall pass through the chambers of his soul,—and if
he is not thus impressed, it will only be because "there is no flesh in
his obdurate heart."*

I have often been utterly astonished, since I came to the north, to
find persons who could speak of the singing, among slaves, as evidence of their contentment and happiness. It is impossible to conceive of a greater mistake. Slaves sing most when they are most
unhappy. The songs of the slave represent the sorrows of his heart;
and he is relieved by them, only as an aching heart is relieved by its
tears. At least, such is my experience. I have often sung to drown my
sorrow, but seldom to express my happiness. Crying for joy, and
singing for joy, were alike uncommon to me while in the jaws of slav-

---

*From *The Task* (1785), by English poet William Cowper (in book 2, "The Time-
Piece.")

ery. The singing of a man cast away upon a desolate island might be as appropriately considered as evidence of contentment and happiness, as the singing of a slave; the songs of the one and of the other are prompted by the same emotion.

CHAPTER III

COLONEL LLOYD KEPT A large and finely cultivated garden, which afforded almost constant employment for four men, besides the chief gardener, (Mr. M'Durmond.) This garden was probably the greatest attraction of the place. During the summer months, people came from far and near—from Baltimore, Easton, and Annapolis—to see it. It abounded in fruits of almost every description, from the hardy apple of the north to the delicate orange of the south. This garden was not the least source of trouble on the plantation. Its excellent fruit was quite a temptation to the hungry swarms of boys, as well as the older slaves, belonging to the colonel, few of whom had the virtue or the vice to resist it. Scarcely a day passed, during the summer, but that some slave had to take the lash for stealing fruit. The colonel had to resort to all kinds of stratagems to keep his slaves out of the garden. The last and most successful one was that of tarring his fence all around; after which, if a slave was caught with any tar upon his person, it was deemed sufficient proof that he had either been into the garden, or had tried to get in. In either case, he was severely whipped by the chief gardener. This plan worked well; the slaves became as fearful of tar as of the lash. They seemed to realize the impossibility of touching *tar* without being defiled.

The colonel also kept a splendid riding equipage. His stable and carriage-house presented the appearance of some of our large city livery establishments. His horses were of the finest form and noblest blood. His carriage-house contained three splendid coaches, three or four gigs, besides dearborns and barouches of the most fashionable style.[19]

This establishment was under the care of two slaves—old Barney and young Barney—father and son. To attend to this establishment was their sole work. But it was by no means an easy employment; for in nothing was Colonel Lloyd more particular than in the management of his horses. The slightest inattention to these was unpardonable, and was visited upon those, under whose care they were placed, with the severest punishment; no excuse could shield them, if the colonel only suspected any want of attention to his horses—a supposition which he frequently indulged, and one which, of course, made the office of old and young Barney a very trying one. They never knew when they were safe from punishment. They were frequently whipped when least deserving, and escaped whipping when most deserving it. Every thing depended upon the looks of the horses, and the state of Colonel Lloyd's own mind when his horses were brought to him for use. If a horse did not move fast enough, or hold his head high enough, it was owing to some fault of his keepers. It was painful to stand near the stable-door, and hear the various complaints against the keepers when a horse was taken out for use. "This horse has not had proper attention. He has not been sufficiently rubbed and curried,* or he has not been properly fed; his food was too wet or too dry; he got it too soon or too late; he was too hot or too cold; he had too much hay, and not enough of grain; or he had too much grain, and not enough of hay; instead of old Barney's attending to the horse, he had very improperly left it to his son." To all these complaints, no matter how unjust, the slave must answer never a word. Colonel Lloyd could not brook† any contradiction from a slave. When he spoke, a slave must stand, listen, and tremble; and such was literally the case. I have seen Colonel Lloyd make old Barney, a man between fifty and sixty years of age, uncover his bald head, kneel down upon the cold, damp ground, and receive upon his naked and toil-worn shoulders more than thirty lashes at the time. Colonel Lloyd had three sons—Edward, Murray, and Daniel,—and three sons-in-law, Mr. Winder, Mr. Nicholson, and Mr. Lowndes. All of these lived at the Great House Farm, and enjoyed the luxury of whipping the servants when they pleased,[20] from old Barney down to William Wilkes, the coach-driver. I have seen Winder make one of the house-servants stand off from him a suitable distance to be touched with the end of his whip, and at every stroke raise great ridges upon his back.

To describe the wealth of Colonel Lloyd would be almost equal to

---

*Brushed with a metallic comb.
†Tolerate.

describing the riches of Job.* He kept from ten to fifteen house-servants. He was said to own a thousand slaves, and I think this estimate
quite within the truth. Colonel Lloyd owned so many that he did not
know them when he saw them; nor did all the slaves of the out-farms
know him. It is reported of him, that, while riding along the road one
day, he met a colored man, and addressed him in the usual manner of
speaking to colored people on the public highways of the south:
"Well, boy, whom do you belong to?" "To Colonel Lloyd," replied the
slave. "Well, does the colonel treat you well?" "No, sir," was the ready
reply. "What, does he work you too hard?" "Yes, sir." "Well, don't he
give you enough to eat?" "Yes, sir, he gives me enough, such as it is."

The colonel, after ascertaining where the slave belonged, rode on;
the man also went on about his business, not dreaming that he had
been conversing with his master. He thought, said, and heard nothing more of the matter, until two or three weeks afterwards. The poor
man was then informed by his overseer that, for having found fault
with his master, he was now to be sold to a Georgia trader. He was
immediately chained and handcuffed; and thus, without a moment's
warning, he was snatched away, and forever sundered,† from his family and friends, by a hand more unrelenting than death. This is the
penalty of telling the truth, of telling the simple truth, in answer to a
series of plain questions.

It is partly in consequence of such facts, that slaves, when inquired
of as to their condition and the character of their masters, almost
universally say they are contented, and that their masters are kind.
The slaveholders have been known to send in spies among their
slaves, to ascertain their views and feelings in regard to their condition. The frequency of this has had the effect to establish among the
slaves the maxim, that a still tongue makes a wise head. They suppress the truth rather than take the consequences of telling it, and in
so doing prove themselves a part of the human family. If they have
any thing to say of their masters, it is generally in their masters' favor,
especially when speaking to an untried man. I have been frequently
asked, when a slave, if I had a kind master, and do not remember ever

*In the Bible, Job is a wealthy patriarch tested by God.
†Separated.

to have given a negative answer; nor did I, in pursuing this course, consider myself as uttering what was absolutely false; for I always measured the kindness of my master by the standard of kindness set up among slaveholders around us. Moreover, slaves are like other people, and imbibe prejudices quite common to others. They think their own better than that of others. Many, under the influence of this prejudice, think their own masters are better than the masters of other slaves; and this, too, in some cases, when the very reverse is true. Indeed, it is not uncommon for slaves even to fall out and quarrel among themselves about the relative goodness of their masters, each contending for the superior goodness of his own over that of the others. At the very same time, they mutually execrate their masters when viewed separately. It was so on our plantation. When Colonel Lloyd's slaves met the slaves of Jacob Jepson, they seldom parted without a quarrel about their masters; Colonel Lloyd's slaves contending that he was the richest, and Mr. Jepson's slaves that he was the smartest, and most of a man. Colonel Lloyd's slaves would boast his ability to buy and sell Jacob Jepson. Mr. Jepson's slaves would boast his ability to whip Colonel Lloyd. These quarrels would almost always end in a fight between the parties, and those that whipped were supposed to have gained the point at issue. They seemed to think that the greatness of their masters was transferable to themselves. It was considered as being bad enough to be a slave; but to be a poor man's slave was deemed a disgrace indeed!

CHAPTER IV

MR. HOPKINS REMAINED BUT a short time in the office of overseer. Why his career was so short, I do not know, but suppose he lacked the necessary severity to suit Colonel Lloyd. Mr. Hopkins was succeeded by Mr. Austin Gore, a man possessing, in an eminent degree, all those traits of character indispensable to what is called a first-rate overseer. Mr. Gore had served Colonel Lloyd, in the capacity of overseer, upon one of the out-farms, and had shown himself worthy of the high station of overseer upon the home or Great House Farm.

Mr. Gore was proud, ambitious, and persevering. He was artful, cruel, and obdurate. He was just the man for such a place, and it was just the place for such a man. It afforded scope for the full exercise of all his powers, and he seemed to be perfectly at home in it. He was one of those who could torture the slightest look, word, or gesture, on the part of the slave, into impudence, and would treat it accordingly. There must be no answering back to him; no explanation was allowed a slave, showing himself to have been wrongfully accused. Mr. Gore acted fully up to the maxim laid down by slaveholders,— "It is better that a dozen slaves suffer under the lash, than that the overseer should be convicted, in the presence of the slaves, of having been at fault." No matter how innocent a slave might be—it availed him nothing, when accused by Mr. Gore of any misdemeanor. To be accused was to be convicted, and to be convicted was to be punished; the one always following the other with immutable certainty. To escape punishment was to escape accusation; and few slaves had the fortune to do either, under the overseership of Mr. Gore. He was just proud enough to demand the most debasing homage of the slave, and quite servile enough to crouch, himself, at the feet of the master. He was ambitious enough to be contented with nothing short of the highest rank of overseers, and persevering enough to reach the height of his ambition. He was cruel enough to inflict the severest punishment, artful enough to descend to the lowest trickery, and obdurate enough to be insensible to the voice of a reproving conscience. He was, of all the overseers, the most dreaded by the slaves. His presence was painful; his eye flashed confusion; and seldom was his sharp, shrill voice heard, without producing horror and trembling in their ranks.

Mr. Gore was a grave man, and, though a young man, he indulged in no jokes, said no funny words, seldom smiled. His words were in perfect keeping with his looks, and his looks were in perfect keeping with his words. Overseers will sometimes indulge in a witty word, even with the slaves; not so with Mr. Gore. He spoke but to command, and commanded but to be obeyed; he dealt sparingly with his words, and bountifully with his whip, never using the former where the latter would answer as well. When he whipped, he seemed to do so from a sense of duty, and feared no consequences. He did nothing reluctantly, no matter how disagreeable; always at his post, never inconsistent. He never promised but to fulfil. He was, in a word, a man of the most inflexible firmness and stone-like coolness.

His savage barbarity was equalled only by the consummate coolness with which he committed the grossest and most savage deeds upon the slaves under his charge. Mr. Gore once undertook to whip one of Colonel Lloyd's slaves, by the name of Demby. He had given Demby but few stripes, when, to get rid of the scourging, he ran and plunged himself into a creek, and stood there at the depth of his shoulders, refusing to come out. Mr. Gore told him that he would give him three calls, and that, if he did not come out at the third call, he would shoot him. The first call was given. Demby made no response, but stood his ground. The second and third calls were given with the same result. Mr. Gore then, without consultation or deliberation with any one, not even giving Demby an additional call, raised his musket to his face, taking deadly aim at his standing victim, and in an instant poor Demby was no more. His mangled body sank out of sight, and blood and brains marked the water where he had stood.

A thrill of horror flashed through every soul upon the plantation, excepting Mr. Gore. He alone seemed cool and collected. He was asked by Colonel Lloyd and my old master, why he resorted to this extraordinary expedient. His reply was, (as well as I can remember,) that Demby had become unmanageable. He was setting a dangerous example to the other slaves,—one which, if suffered to pass without some such demonstration on his part, would finally lead to the total subversion of all rule and order upon the plantation. He argued that if one slave refused to be corrected, and escaped with his life, the other slaves would soon copy the example; the result of which would be, the freedom of the slaves, and the enslavement of the whites. Mr. Gore's defence was satisfactory. He was continued in his station as overseer upon the home plantation. His fame as an overseer went abroad. His horrid crime was not even submitted to judicial investigation. It was committed in the presence of slaves, and they of course could neither institute a suit, nor testify against him; and thus the guilty perpetrator of one of the bloodiest and most foul murders goes unwhipped of justice, and uncensured by the community in which he lives. Mr. Gore lived in St. Michael's, Talbot county, Maryland, when I left there; and if he is still alive, he very probably lives there now; and if so, he is now, as he was then, as highly esteemed and as much respected as though his guilty soul had not been stained with his brother's blood.

I speak advisedly when I say this,—that killing a slave, or any colored person, in Talbot county, Maryland, is not treated as a crime, either by the courts or the community. Mr. Thomas Lanman, of St. Michael's, killed two slaves, one of whom he killed with a hatchet, by knocking his brains out. He used to boast of the commission of the awful and bloody deed. I have heard him do so laughingly, saying, among other things, that he was the only benefactor of his country in the company, and that when others would do as much as he had done, we should be relieved of "the d——d niggers."

The wife of Mr. Giles Hick, living but a short distance from where I used to live, murdered my wife's cousin, a young girl between fifteen and sixteen years of age, mangling her person in the most horrible manner, breaking her nose and breastbone with a stick, so that the poor girl expired in a few hours afterward. She was immediately buried, but had not been in her untimely grave but a few hours before she was taken up and examined by the coroner, who decided that she had come to her death by severe beating. The offence for which this girl was thus murdered was this:—She had been set that night to mind Mrs. Hick's baby, and during the night she fell asleep, and the baby cried. She, having lost her rest for several nights previous, did not hear the crying. They were both in the room with Mrs.

Hicks. Mrs. Hicks, finding the girl slow to move, jumped from her bed, seized an oak stick of wood by the fireplace, and with it broke the girl's nose and breastbone, and thus ended her life. I will not say that this most horrid murder produced no sensation in the community. It did produce sensation, but not enough to bring the murderess to punishment. There was a warrant issued for her arrest, but it was never served. Thus she escaped not only punishment, but even the pain of being arraigned* before a court for her horrid crime.

Whilst I am detailing bloody deeds which took place during my stay on Colonel Lloyd's plantation, I will briefly narrate another, which occurred about the same time as the murder of Demby by Mr. Gore.

Colonel Lloyd's slaves were in the habit of spending a part of their nights and Sundays in fishing for oysters, and in this way made up the deficiency of their scanty allowance. An old man belonging to Colonel Lloyd, while thus engaged, happened to get beyond the limits of Colonel Lloyd's, and on the premises of Mr. Beal Bondly. At this trespass, Mr. Bondly took offence, and with his musket came down to the shore, and blew its deadly contents into the poor old man.

Mr. Bondly came over to see Colonel Lloyd the next day, whether to pay him for his property, or to justify himself in what he had done, I know not. At any rate, this whole fiendish transaction was soon hushed up. There was very little said about it at all, and nothing done. It was a common saying, even among little white boys, that it was worth a half-cent to kill a "nigger," and a half-cent to bury one.

---

*Brought into court to answer a criminal charge.

CHAPTER V

As to my own treatment while I lived on Colonel Lloyd's plantation, it was very similar to that of the other slave children. I was not old enough to work in the field, and there being little else than field work to do, I had a great deal of leisure time. The most I had to do was to drive up the cows at evening, keep the fowls out of the garden, keep the front yard clean, and run of errands for my old master's daughter, Mrs. Lucretia Auld. The most of my leisure time I spent in helping Master Daniel Lloyd in finding his birds, after he had shot them. My connection with Master Daniel was of some advantage to me. He became quite attached to me, and was a sort of protector of me. He would not allow the older boys to impose upon me, and would divide his cakes with me.

I was seldom whipped by my old master, and suffered little from any thing else than hunger and cold. I suffered much from hunger, but much more from cold. In hottest summer and coldest winter, I was kept almost naked—no shoes, no stockings, no jacket, no trousers, nothing on but a coarse tow linen shirt, reaching only to my knees. I had no bed. I must have perished with cold, but that, the coldest nights, I used to steal a bag which was used for carrying corn to the mill. I would crawl into this bag, and there sleep on the cold, damp, clay floor, with my head in and feet out. My feet have been so cracked with the frost, that the pen with which I am writing might be laid in the gashes.[21]

We were not regularly allowanced. Our food was coarse corn meal boiled. This was called *mush*. It was put into a large wooden tray or trough, and set down upon the ground. The children were then called, like so many pigs, and like so many pigs they would come and devour the mush; some with oystershells, others with pieces of shingle, some with naked hands, and none with spoons. He that ate fastest got most; he that was strongest secured the best place; and few left the trough satisfied.

I was probably between seven and eight years old when I left

Colonel Lloyd's plantation. I left it with joy. I shall never forget the ecstasy with which I received the intelligence that my old master (Anthony) had determined to let me go to Baltimore, to live with Mr. Hugh Auld, brother to my old master's son-in-law, Captain Thomas Auld. I received this information about three days before my departure. They were three of the happiest days I ever enjoyed. I spent the most part of all these three days in the creek, washing off the plantation scurf,* and preparing myself for my departure.[22]

The pride of appearance which this would indicate was not my own. I spent the time in washing, not so much because I wished to, but because Mrs. Lucretia had told me I must get all the dead skin off my feet and knees before I could go to Baltimore; for the people in Baltimore were very cleanly, and would laugh at me if I looked dirty. Besides, she was going to give me a pair of trousers, which I should not put on unless I got all the dirt off me. The thought of owning a pair of trousers was great indeed! It was almost a sufficient motive, not only to make me take off what would be called by pig-drovers† the mange,‡ but the skin itself. I went at it in good earnest, working for the first time with the hope of reward.

The ties that ordinarily bind children to their homes were all suspended in my case. I found no severe trial in my departure. My home was charmless; it was not home to me; on parting from it, I could not feel that I was leaving any thing which I could have enjoyed by staying. My mother was dead, my grandmother lived far off, so that I seldom saw her. I had two sisters and one brother, that lived in the same house with me; but the early separation of us from our mother had well nigh blotted the fact of our relationship from our memories. I looked for home elsewhere, and was confident of finding none which I should relish less than the one which I was leaving. If, however, I found in my new home hardship, hunger, whipping, and nakedness, I had the consolation that I should not have escaped any one of them by staying. Having already had more than a taste of them in the house of my old master, and having endured them there, I very naturally inferred my ability to endure them elsewhere, and especially at

---

*Dry, scaly skin.
†Those who drive pigs to market.
‡Scab or itch in pigs, dogs, and other animals.

Baltimore; for I had something of the feeling about Baltimore that is
expressed in the proverb, that "being hanged in England is preferable
to dying a natural death in Ireland." I had the strongest desire to see
Baltimore. Cousin Tom, though not fluent in speech, had inspired
me with that desire by his eloquent description of the place. I could
never point out any thing at the Great House, no matter how beautiful or powerful, but that he had seen something at Baltimore far ex-
ceeding, both in beauty and strength, the object which I pointed out
to him. Even the Great House itself, with all its pictures, was far in-
ferior to many buildings in Baltimore. So strong was my desire, that
I thought a gratification of it would fully compensate for whatever
loss of comforts I should sustain by the exchange. I left without a regret, and with the highest hopes of future happiness.

We sailed out of Miles River for Baltimore on a Saturday morning. I remember only the day of the week, for at that time I had no
knowledge of the days of the month, nor the months of the year. On
setting sail, I walked aft,* and gave to Colonel Lloyd's plantation
what I hoped would be the last look. I then placed myself in the
bows† of the sloop, and there spent the remainder of the day in looking ahead, interesting myself in what was in the distance rather than
in things near by or behind.

In the afternoon of that day, we reached Annapolis, the capital of
the State. We stopped but a few moments, so that I had no time to
go on shore. It was the first large town that I had ever seen, and
though it would look small compared with some of our New England factory villages, I thought it a wonderful place for its size—
more imposing even than the Great House Farm!

We arrived at Baltimore early on Sunday morning, landing at
Smith's Wharf, not far from Bowley's Wharf. We had on board the
sloop a large flock of sheep; and after aiding in driving them to the
slaughterhouse of Mr. Curtis on Louden Slater's Hill, I was conducted
by Rich, one of the hands belonging on board of the sloop, to my new
home in Alliciana Street, near Mr. Gardner's ship-yard, on Fells Point.

Mr. and Mrs. Auld were both at home, and met me at the door
with their little son Thomas, to take care of whom I had been given.

---

*To the rear of the boat.
†Rounded sides at the forward end of a boat.

And here I saw what I had never seen before; it was a white face beaming with the most kindly emotions; it was the face of my new mistress, Sophia Auld. I wish I could describe the rapture that flashed through my soul as I beheld it. It was a new and strange sight to me, brightening up my pathway with the light of happiness. Little Thomas was told, there was his Freddy,—and I was told to take care of little Thomas; and thus I entered upon the duties of my new home with the most cheering prospect ahead.

I look upon my departure from Colonel Lloyd's plantation as one of the most interesting events of my life. It is possible, and even quite probable, that but for the mere circumstance of being removed from that plantation to Baltimore, I should have to-day, instead of being here seated by my own table, in the enjoyment of freedom and the happiness of home, writing this Narrative, been confined in the galling chains of slavery. Going to live at Baltimore laid the foundation, and opened the gateway, to all my subsequent prosperity. I have ever regarded it as the first plain manifestation of that kind providence which has ever since attended me, and marked my life with so many favors. I regarded the selection of myself as being somewhat remarkable. There were a number of slave children that might have been sent from the plantation to Baltimore. There were those younger, those older, and those of the same age. I was chosen from among them all, and was the first, last, and only choice.

I may be deemed superstitious, and even egotistical, in regarding this event as a special interposition of divine Providence in my favor. But I should be false to the earliest sentiments of my soul, if I suppressed the opinion. I prefer to be true to myself, even at the hazard of incurring the ridicule of others, rather than to be false, and incur my own abhorrence. From my earliest recollection, I date the entertainment of a deep conviction that slavery would not always be able to hold me within its foul embrace; and in the darkest hours of my career in slavery, this living word of faith and spirit of hope departed not from me, but remained like ministering angels to cheer me through the gloom. This good spirit was from God, and to him I offer thanksgiving and praise.

CHAPTER VI

MY NEW MISTRESS PROVED to be all she appeared when I first met her at the door,—a woman of the kindest heart and finest feelings. She had never had a slave under her control previously to myself, and prior to her marriage she had been dependent upon her own industry for a living. She was by trade a weaver; and by constant application to her business, she had been in a good degree preserved from the blighting and dehumanizing effects of slavery. I was utterly astonished at her goodness. I scarcely knew how to behave towards her. She was entirely unlike any other white woman I had ever seen. I could not approach her as I was accustomed to approach other white ladies. My early instruction was all out of place. The crouching servility, usually so acceptable a quality in a slave, did not answer when manifested toward her. Her favor was not gained by it; she seemed to be disturbed by it. She did not deem it impudent or unmannerly for a slave to look her in the face. The meanest slave was put fully at ease in her presence, and none left without feeling better for having seen her. Her face was made of heavenly smiles, and her voice of tranquil music.

But, alas! this kind heart had but a short time to remain such. The fatal poison of irresponsible power was already in her hands, and soon commenced its infernal work. That cheerful eye, under the influence of slavery, soon became red with rage; that voice, made all of sweet accord, changed to one of harsh and horrid discord; and that angelic face gave place to that of a demon.

Very soon after I went to live with Mr. and Mrs. Auld, she very kindly commenced to teach me the A, B, C. After I had learned this, she assisted me in learning to spell words of three or four letters. Just at this point of my progress, Mr. Auld found out what was going on, and at once forbade Mrs. Auld to instruct me further, telling her, among other things, that it was unlawful, as well as unsafe, to teach a slave to read. To use his own words further, he said, "If you give a nigger an inch, he will take an ell.* A nigger should know nothing but to obey his master—to do as he is told to do. Learning would *spoil* the best nigger in the world. Now," said he, "if you teach that nigger (speaking of myself) how to read, there would be no keeping him. It would forever unfit him to be a slave. He would at once become unmanageable, and of no value to his master. As to himself, it could do him no good, but a great deal of harm. It would make him discontented and unhappy." These words sank deep into my heart, stirred up sentiments within that lay slumbering, and called into existence an entirely new train of thought. It was a new and special revelation, explaining dark and mysterious things, with which my youthful understanding had struggled, but struggled in vain. I now understood what had been to me a most perplexing difficulty—to wit, the white man's power to enslave the black man. It was a grand achievement, and I prized it highly. From that moment, I understood the pathway from slavery to freedom. It was just what I wanted, and I got it at a time when I the least expected it. Whilst I was saddened by the thought of losing the aid of my kind mistress, I was gladdened by the invaluable instruction which, by the merest accident, I had gained from my master. Though conscious of the difficulty of learning without a teacher, I set out with high hope, and a fixed purpose, at whatever cost of trouble, to learn how to read. The very decided manner with which he spoke, and strove to impress his wife with the evil consequences of giving me instruction, served to convince me that he was deeply sensible of the truths he was uttering. It gave me the best assurance that I might rely with the utmost confidence on the results which, he said, would flow from teaching me to read. What he most dreaded, that I most desired. What he most loved, that I most hated. That which to him was a great evil, to be carefully shunned, was to me a great good, to be diligently sought; and the argument which he so warmly urged, against my learning to read, only served to inspire me with a desire and determination to learn. In learning to read, I owe almost as much to the bitter opposition of my master, as to the kindly aid of my mistress. I acknowledge the benefit of both.

I had resided but a short time in Baltimore[23] before I observed a marked difference, in the treatment of slaves, from that which I had

---

*Old unit of length, varying in different countries; the English ell was 45 inches.

witnessed in the country. A city slave is almost a freeman, compared with a slave on the plantation. He is much better fed and clothed, and enjoys privileges altogether unknown to the slave on the plantation. There is a vestige of decency, a sense of shame, that does much to curb and check those outbreaks of atrocious cruelty so commonly enacted upon the plantation. He is a desperate slaveholder, who will shock the humanity of his nonslaveholding neighbors with the cries of his lacerated slave. Few are willing to incur the odium attaching to the reputation of being a cruel master; and above all things, they would not be known as not giving a slave enough to eat. Every city slaveholder is anxious to have it known of him, that he feeds his slaves well; and it is due to them to say, that most of them do give their slaves enough to eat. There are, however, some painful exceptions to this rule. Directly opposite to us, on Philpot Street, lived Mr. Thomas Hamilton. He owned two slaves. Their names were Henrietta and Mary. Henrietta was about twenty-two years of age, Mary was about fourteen; and of all the mangled and emaciated creatures I ever looked upon, these two were the most so. His heart must be harder than stone, that could look upon these unmoved. The head, neck, and shoulders of Mary were literally cut to pieces. I have frequently felt her head, and found it nearly covered with festering sores, caused by the lash of her cruel mistress. I do not know that her master ever whipped her, but I have been an eyewitness to the cruelty of Mrs. Hamilton. I used to be in Mr. Hamilton's house nearly every day. Mrs. Hamilton used to sit in a large chair in the middle of the room, with a heavy cowskin always by her side, and scarce an hour passed during the day but was marked by the blood of one of these slaves. The girls seldom passed her without her saying, "Move faster, you *black gip!*"* at the same time giving them a blow with the cowskin over the head or shoulders, often drawing the blood. She would then say, "Take that, you *black gip!*"—continuing, "If you don't move faster, I'll move you!" Added to the cruel lashings to which these slaves were subjected, they were kept nearly half-starved. They seldom knew what it was to eat a full meal. I have seen Mary contending with the pigs for the offal† thrown into the street. So much was Mary kicked and cut to pieces, that she was oftener called "*pecked*" than by her name.

---

*Gypsy.
†Waste or by-products of slaughtered or dead animals.

CHAPTER VII

I LIVED IN MASTER Hugh's family about seven years. During this time, I succeeded in learning to read and write. In accomplishing this, I was compelled to resort to various stratagems. I had no regular teacher. My mistress, who had kindly commenced to instruct me, had, in compliance with the advice and direction of her husband, not only ceased to instruct, but had set her face against my being instructed by any one else. It is due, however, to my mistress to say of her, that she did not adopt this course of treatment immediately. She at first lacked the depravity indispensable to shutting me up in mental darkness. It was at least necessary for her to have some training in the exercise of irresponsible power, to make her equal to the task of treating me as though I were a brute.

My mistress was, as I have said, a kind and tender-hearted woman; and in the simplicity of her soul she commenced, when I first went to live with her, to treat me as she supposed one human being ought to treat another. In entering upon the duties of a slaveholder, she did not seem to perceive that I sustained to her the relation of a mere chattel, and that for her to treat me as a human being was not only wrong, but dangerously so. Slavery proved as injurious to her as it did to me.[24] When I went there, she was a pious, warm, and tender-hearted woman. There was no sorrow or suffering for which she had not a tear. She had bread for the hungry, clothes for the naked, and comfort for every mourner that came within her reach. Slavery soon proved its ability to divest her of these heavenly qualities. Under its influence, the tender heart became stone, and the lamb-like disposition gave way to one of tiger-like fierceness. The first step in her downward course was in her ceasing to instruct me. She now commenced to practise her husband's precepts. She finally became even more violent in her opposition than her husband himself. She was not satisfied with simply doing as well as he had commanded; she seemed anxious to do better. Nothing seemed to make her more angry than to see me with a newspaper. She seemed to think that here lay the danger. I have had her rush at me with a face made all up of fury, and snatch from me a newspaper, in a manner that fully revealed her apprehension. She was an apt woman; and a little experience soon demonstrated, to her satisfaction, that education and slavery were incompatible with each other.

From this time I was most narrowly watched. If I was in a separate room any considerable length of time, I was sure to be suspected of having a book, and was at once called to give an account of myself. All this, however, was too late. The first step had been taken. Mistress, in teaching me the alphabet, had given me the *inch*, and no precaution could prevent me from taking the *ell*.

The plan which I adopted, and the one by which I was most successful, was that of making friends of all the little white boys whom I met in the street. As many of these as I could, I converted into teachers. With their kindly aid, obtained at different times and in different places, I finally succeeded in learning to read. When I was sent of errands, I always took my book with me, and by going one part of my errand quickly, I found time to get a lesson before my return. I used also to carry bread with me, enough of which was always in the house, and to which I was always welcome; for I was much better off in this regard than many of the poor white children in our neighborhood. This bread I used to bestow upon the hungry little urchins, who, in return, would give me that more valuable bread of knowledge. I am strongly tempted to give the names of two or three of those little boys, as a testimonial of the gratitude and affection I bear them; but prudence forbids;—not that it would injure me, but it might embarrass them; for it is almost an unpardonable offence to teach slaves to read in this Christian country. It is enough to say of the dear little fellows, that they lived on Philpot Street, very near Durgin and Bailey's shipyard. I used to talk this matter of slavery over with them. I would sometimes say to them, I wished I could be as free as they would be when they got to be men. "You will be free as soon as you are twenty-one, *but I am a slave for life!* Have not I as good a right to be free as you have?" These words used to trouble them; they would express for me the liveliest sympathy, and console me with the hope that something would occur by which I might be free.

I was now about twelve years old, and the thought of being *a slave for life* began to bear heavily upon my heart. Just about this time, I got hold of a book entitled "The Columbian Orator."[25] Every opportunity I got, I used to read this book. Among much of other interesting matter, I found in it a dialogue between a master and his slave. The slave was represented as having run away from his master three times. The dialogue represented the conversation which took place between them, when the slave was retaken the third time. In this dialogue, the whole argument in behalf of slavery was brought forward by the master, all of which was disposed of by the slave. The slave was made to say some very smart as well as impressive things in reply to his master—things which had the desired though unexpected effect; for the conversation resulted in the voluntary emancipation of the slave on the part of the master.

In the same book, I met with one of Sheridan's mighty speeches on and in behalf of Catholic emancipation.[26] These were choice documents to me. I read them over and over again with unabated interest. They gave tongue to interesting thoughts of my own soul, which had frequently flashed through my mind, and died away for want of utterance. The moral which I gained from the dialogue was the power of truth over the conscience of even a slaveholder. What I got from Sheridan was a bold denunciation of slavery, and a powerful vindication of human rights. The reading of these documents enabled me to utter my thoughts, and to meet the arguments brought forward to sustain slavery; but while they relieved me of one difficulty, they brought on another even more painful than the one of which I was relieved. The more I read, the more I was led to abhor and detest my enslavers. I could regard them in no other light than a band of successful robbers, who had left their homes, and gone to Africa, and stolen us from our homes, and in a strange land reduced us to slavery. I loathed them as being the meanest as well as the most wicked of men. As I read and contemplated the subject, behold! that very discontentment which Master Hugh had predicted would follow my learning to read had already come, to torment and sting my soul to unutterable anguish. As I writhed under it, I would at times feel that learning to read had been a curse rather than a blessing. It had given me a view of my wretched condition, without the remedy. It opened my eyes to the horrible pit, but to no ladder upon which to get out. In moments of agony, I envied my fellow-slaves for their stupidity. I have often wished myself a beast. I preferred the condition

of the meanest reptile to my own. Any thing, no matter what, to get
rid of thinking! It was this everlasting thinking of my condition that
tormented me. There was no getting rid of it. It was pressed upon me
by every object within sight or hearing, animate or inanimate. The
silver trump of freedom had roused my soul to eternal wakefulness.
Freedom now appeared, to disappear no more forever. It was heard in
every sound, and seen in every thing. It was ever present to torment
me with a sense of my wretched condition. I saw nothing without
seeing it, I heard nothing without hearing it, and felt nothing without feeling it. It looked from every star, it smiled in every calm,
breathed in every wind, and moved in every storm.

I often found myself regretting my own existence, and wishing
myself dead; and but for the hope of being free, I have no doubt but
that I should have killed myself, or done something for which I
should have been killed. While in this state of mind, I was eager to
hear any one speak of slavery. I was a ready listener. Every little while,
I could hear something about the abolitionists. It was some time before I found what the word meant. It was always used in such con-
nections as to make it an interesting word to me. If a slave ran away
and succeeded in getting clear, or if a slave killed his master, set fire
to a barn, or did any thing very wrong in the mind of a slaveholder,
it was spoken of as the fruit of *abolition*.[27] Hearing the word in this
connection very often, I set about learning what it meant. The dictionary afforded me little or no help. I found it was "the act of abolishing;" but then I did not know what was to be abolished. Here I
was perplexed. I did not dare to ask any one about its meaning, for I
was satisfied that it was something they wanted me to know very little about. After a patient waiting, I got one of our city papers, containing an account of the number of petitions from the north,
praying for the abolition of slavery in the District of Columbia, and
of the slave trade between the States. From this time I understood
the words *abolition* and *abolitionist*, and always drew near when that
word was spoken, expecting to hear something of importance to myself and fellow-slaves. The light broke in upon me by degrees. I went
one day down on the wharf of Mr. Waters; and seeing two Irishmen
unloading a scow* of stone, I went, unasked, and helped them. When

---

*Large, flat-bottomed boat designed for moving heavy cargo.

we had finished, one of them came to me and asked me if I were a slave. I told him I was. He asked, "Are ye a slave for life?" I told him that I was. The good Irishman seemed to be deeply affected by the statement. He said to the other that it was a pity so fine a little fellow as myself should be a slave for life. He said it was a shame to hold me. They both advised me to run away to the north; that I should find friends there, and that I should be free. I pretended not to be interested in what they said, and treated them as if I did not understand them; for I feared they might be treacherous. White men have been known to encourage slaves to escape, and then, to get the reward, catch them and return them to their masters. I was afraid that these seemingly good men might use me so; but I nevertheless remembered their advice, and from that time I resolved to run away. I looked forward to a time at which it would be safe for me to escape. I was too young to think of doing so immediately; besides, I wished to learn how to write, as I might have occasion to write my own pass. I consoled myself with the hope that I should one day find a good chance. Meanwhile, I would learn to write.

The idea as to how I might learn to write was suggested to me by being in Durgin and Bailey's ship-yard, and frequently seeing the ship carpenters, after hewing, and getting a piece of timber ready for use, write on the timber the name of that part of the ship for which it was intended. When a piece of timber was intended for the larboard side,* it would be marked thus—"L." When a piece was for the starboard side, it would be marked thus—"S." A piece for the larboard side forward, would be marked thus—"L.F." When a piece was for starboard side forward, it would be marked thus—"S.F." For larboard aft, it would be marked thus—"L.A." For starboard aft, it would be marked thus—"S.A." I soon learned the names of these letters, and for what they were intended when placed upon a piece of timber in the ship-yard. I immediately commenced copying them, and in a short time was able to make the four letters named. After that, when I met with any boy who I knew could write, I would tell him I could write as well as he. The next word would be, "I don't believe you. Let me see you try it." I would then make the letters which

---

*Looking forward on a ship, the larboard, or port, side is to the left and the starboard side is to the right.

I had been so fortunate as to learn, and ask him to beat that. In this way I got a good many lessons in writing, which it is quite possible I should never have gotten in any other way. During this time, my copy-book was the board fence, brick wall, and pavement; my pen and ink was a lump of chalk. With these, I learned mainly how to write. I then commenced and continued copying the Italics in Webster's Spelling Book,* until I could make them all without looking on the book. By this time, my little Master Thomas had gone to school, and learned how to write, and had written over a number of copybooks. These had been brought home, and shown to some of our near neighbors, and then laid aside. My mistress used to go to class meeting† at the Wilk Street meetinghouse every Monday afternoon, and leave me to take care of the house. When left thus, I used to spend the time in writing in the spaces left in Master Thomas's copybook, copying what he had written. I continued to do this until I could write a hand very similar to that of Master Thomas. Thus, after a long, tedious effort for years, I finally succeeded in learning how to write.

---

*The *Elementary Spelling Book* (1783) by American lexicographer Noah Webster.
†Church.

CHAPTER VIII

IN A VERY SHORT time after I went to live at Baltimore, my old master's youngest son Richard died; and in about three years and six months after his death, my old master, Captain Anthony, died, leaving only his son, Andrew, and daughter, Lucretia, to share his estate. He died while on a visit to see his daughter at Hillsborough. Cut off thus unexpectedly, he left no will as to the disposal of his property. It was therefore necessary to have a valuation of the property, that it might be equally divided between Mrs. Lucretia and Master Andrew. I was immediately sent for, to be valued with the other property. Here again my feelings rose up in detestation of slavery. I had now a new conception of my degraded condition. Prior to this, I had become, if not insensible to my lot, at least partly so. I left Baltimore with a young heart overborne with sadness, and a soul full of apprehension. I took passage with Captain Rowe, in the schooner Wild Cat, and, after a sail of about twenty-four hours, I found myself near the place of my birth. I had now been absent from it almost, if not quite, five years. I, however, remembered the place very well. I was only about five years old when I left it, to go and live with my old master on Colonel Lloyd's plantation; so that I was now between ten and eleven years old.

We were all ranked together at the valuation. Men and women, old and young, married and single, were ranked with horses, sheep, and swine. There were horses and men, cattle and women, pigs and children, all holding the same rank in the scale of being, and were all subjected to the same narrow examination. Silvery-headed age and sprightly youth, maids and matrons, had to undergo the same indelicate inspection. At this moment, I saw more clearly than ever the brutalizing effects of slavery upon both slave and slaveholder.

After the valuation, then came the division. I have no language to express the high excitement and deep anxiety which were felt among us poor slaves during this time. Our fate for life was now to be decided. We had no more voice in that decision than the brutes among

49

whom we were ranked. A single word from the white men was enough—against all our wishes, prayers, and entreaties—to sunder forever the dearest friends, dearest kindred, and strongest ties known to human beings. In addition to the pain of separation, there was the horrid dread of falling into the hands of Master Andrew. He was known to us all as being a most cruel wretch,—a common drunkard, who had, by his reckless mismanagement and profligate dissipation, already wasted a large portion of his father's property. We all felt that we might as well be sold at once to the Georgia traders, as to pass into his hands; for we knew that that would be our inevitable condition,—a condition held by us all in the utmost horror and dread.

I suffered more anxiety than most of my fellow-slaves. I had known what it was to be kindly treated; they had known nothing of the kind. They had seen little or nothing of the world. They were in very deed men and women of sorrow, and acquainted with grief. Their backs had been made familiar with the bloody lash, so that they had become callous; mine was yet tender; for while at Baltimore I got few whippings, and few slaves could boast of a kinder master and mistress than myself; and the thought of passing out of their hands into those of Master Andrew—a man who, but a few days before, to give me a sample of his bloody disposition, took my little brother by the throat, threw him on the ground, and with the heel of his boot stamped upon his head till the blood gushed from his nose and ears—was well calculated to make me anxious as to my fate. After he had committed this savage outrage upon my brother, he turned to me, and said that was the way he meant to serve me one of these days,—meaning, I suppose, when I came into his possession.

Thanks to a kind Providence, I fell to the portion of Mrs. Lucretia, and was sent immediately back to Baltimore, to live again in the family of Master Hugh. Their joy at my return equalled their sorrow at my departure. It was a glad day to me. I had escaped a worse than lion's jaws. I was absent from Baltimore, for the purpose of valuation and division, just about one month, and it seemed to have been six.

Very soon after my return to Baltimore, my mistress, Lucretia, died, leaving her husband and one child, Amanda; and in a very short time after her death, Master Andrew died. Now all the property of my old master, slaves included, was in the hands of strangers,—strangers who had had nothing to do with accumulating it. Not a slave was left free. All remained slaves, from the youngest to the old-est. If any one thing in my experience, more than another, served to deepen my conviction of the infernal character of slavery, and to fill me with unutterable loathing of slaveholders, it was their base in-gratitude to my poor old grandmother. She had served my old mas-ter faithfully from youth to old age. She had been the source of all his wealth; she had peopled his plantation with slaves; she had become a great grandmother in his service. She had rocked him in infancy, at-tended him in childhood, served him through life, and at his death wiped from his icy brow the cold death-sweat, and closed his eyes forever. She was nevertheless left a slave—a slave for life—a slave in the hands of strangers; and in their hands she saw her children, her grandchildren, and her great-grandchildren, divided, like so many sheep,[28] without being gratified with the small privilege of a single word, as to their or her own destiny. And, to cap the climax of their base ingratitude and fiendish barbarity, my grandmother, who was now very old, having outlived my old master and all his children, having seen the beginning and end of all of them, and her present owners finding she was of but little value, her frame already racked with the pains of old age, and complete helplessness fast stealing over her once active limbs, they took her to the woods, built her a little hut, put up a little mud-chimney, and then made her welcome to the privilege of supporting herself there in perfect loneliness; thus virtu-ally turning her out to die! If my poor old grandmother now lives, she lives to suffer in utter loneliness; she lives to remember and mourn over the loss of children, the loss of grandchildren, and the loss of great-grandchildren. They are, in the language of the slave's poet, Whittier,—

> Gone, gone, sold and gone
> To the rice swamp dank and lone,
> Where the slave-whip ceaseless swings,
> Where the noisome* insect stings,
> Where the fever-demon strews
> Poison with the falling dews,
> Where the sickly sunbeams glare

---

*Offensive; harmful.

> Through the hot and misty air:—
> Gone, gone, sold and gone
> To the rice swamp dank and lone,
> From Virginia hills and waters—
> Woe is me, my stolen daughters!*

The hearth is desolate. The children, the unconscious children, who once sang and danced in her presence, are gone. She gropes her way, in the darkness of age, for a drink of water. Instead of the voices of her children, she hears by day the moans of the dove, and by night the screams of the hideous owl. All is gloom. The grave is at the door. And now, when weighed down by the pains and aches of old age, when the head inclines to the feet, when the beginning and ending of human existence meet, and helpless infancy and painful old age combine together—at this time, this most needful time, the time for the exercise of that tenderness and affection which children only can exercise towards a declining parent—my poor old grandmother, the devoted mother of twelve children, is left all alone, in yonder little hut, before a few dim embers. She stands—she sits—she staggers—she falls—she groans—she dies—and there are none of her children or grandchildren present, to wipe from her wrinkled brow the cold sweat of death, or to place beneath the sod her fallen remains. Will not a righteous God visit for these things?†

In about two years after the death of Mrs. Lucretia, Master Thomas married his second wife. Her name was Rowena Hamilton. She was the eldest daughter of Mr. William Hamilton. Master now lived in St. Michael's.[29] Not long after his marriage, a misunderstanding took place between himself and Master Hugh; and as a means of punishing his brother, he took me from him to live with himself at St. Michael's. Here I underwent another most painful separation. It, however, was not so severe as the one I dreaded at the division of property; for, during this interval, a great change had taken place in Master Hugh and his once kind and affectionate wife. The influence of brandy upon him, and of slavery upon her, had effected

---

*From "The Farewell," by American poet and abolitionist John Greenleaf Whittier (1807–1892).
†Reference to the Bible, Jeremiah 5:29.

a disastrous change in the characters of both; so that, as far as they were concerned, I thought I had little to lose by the change. But it was not to them that I was attached. It was to those little Baltimore boys that I felt the strongest attachment. I had received many good lessons from them, and was still receiving them, and the thought of leaving them was painful indeed. I was leaving, too, without the hope of ever being allowed to return. Master Thomas had said he would never let me return again. The barrier betwixt himself and brother he considered impassable.

I then had to regret that I did not at least make the attempt to carry out my resolution to run away; for the chances of success are tenfold greater from the city than from the country.

I sailed from Baltimore for St. Michael's in the sloop Amanda, Captain Edward Dodson. On my passage, I paid particular attention to the direction which the steamboats took to go to Philadelphia. I found, instead of going down, on reaching North Point they went up the bay, in a north-easterly direction. I deemed this knowledge of the utmost importance. My determination to run away was again revived. I resolved to wait only so long as the offering of a favorable opportunity. When that came, I was determined to be off.

CHAPTER IX

I HAVE NOW REACHED a period of my life when I can give dates. I left Baltimore, and went to live with Master Thomas Auld, at St. Michael's, in March, 1832. It was now more than seven years since I lived with him in the family of my old master, on Colonel Lloyd's plantation. We of course were now almost entire strangers to each other. He was to me a new master, and I to him a new slave. I was ignorant of his temper and disposition; he was equally so of mine. A very short time, however, brought us into full acquaintance with each other. I was made acquainted with his wife not less than with himself. They were well matched, being equally mean and cruel. I was now, for the first time during a space of more than seven years, made to feel the painful gnawings of hunger—a something which I had not experienced before since I left Colonel Lloyd's plantation. It went hard enough with me then, when I could look back to no period at which I had enjoyed a sufficiency. It was tenfold harder after living in Master Hugh's family, where I had always had enough to eat, and of that which was good. I have said Master Thomas was a mean man. He was so. Not to give a slave enough to eat, is regarded as the most aggravated development of meanness even among slaveholders. The rule is, no matter how coarse the food, only let there be enough of it. This is the theory; and in the part of Maryland from which I came, it is the general practice,—though there are many exceptions. Master Thomas gave us enough of neither coarse nor fine food. There were four slaves of us in the kitchen—my sister Eliza, my aunt Priscilla, Henny, and myself; and we were allowed less than a half of a bushel of corn-meal per week, and very little else, either in the shape of meat or vegetables. It was not enough for us to subsist upon. We were therefore reduced to the wretched necessity of living at the expense of our neighbors. This we did by begging and stealing, whichever came handy in the time of need, the one being considered as legitimate as the other. A great many times have we poor creatures been nearly perishing with hunger, when food in abundance lay mouldering in the safe* and smoke-house, and our pious mistress was aware of the fact; and yet that mistress and her husband would kneel every morning, and pray that God would bless them in basket and store!

Bad as all slaveholders are, we seldom meet one destitute of every element of character commanding respect. My master was one of this rare sort. I do not know of one single noble act ever performed by him. The leading trait in his character was meanness; and if there were any other element in his nature, it was made subject to this. He was mean; and, like most other mean men, he lacked the ability to conceal his meanness. Captain Auld was not born a slaveholder. He had been a poor man, master only of a Bay craft. He came into possession of all his slaves by marriage; and of all men, adopted slaveholders are the worst. He was cruel, but cowardly. He commanded without firmness. In the enforcement of his rules, he was at times rigid, and at times lax. At times, he spoke to his slaves with the firmness of Napoleon and the fury of a demon; at other times, he might well be mistaken for an inquirer who had lost his way. He did nothing of himself. He might have passed for a lion, but for his ears. In all things noble which he attempted, his own meanness shone most conspicuous. His airs, words, and actions, were the airs, words, and actions of born slaveholders, and, being assumed, were awkward enough. He was not even a good imitator. He possessed all the disposition to deceive, but wanted the power. Having no resources within himself, he was compelled to be the copyist of many, and being such, he was forever the victim of inconsistency; and of consequence he was an object of contempt, and was held as such even by his slaves. The luxury of having slaves of his own to wait upon him was something new and unprepared for. He was a slaveholder without the ability to hold slaves. He found himself incapable of managing his slaves either by force, fear, or fraud. We seldom called him "master;" we generally called him "Captain Auld," and were hardly disposed to title him at all. I doubt not that our conduct had much to do with making him appear awkward, and of consequence fretful. Our want of reverence for him must have perplexed him greatly. He wished to have us call him master, but lacked the firmness necessary to command us to do so. His wife used to insist

---

*Cooled compartment for storing perishable food.

upon our calling him so, but to no purpose. In August, 1832, my master attended a Methodist camp-meeting* held in the Bay-side, Talbot
county, and there experienced religion. I indulged a faint hope that his
conversion would lead him to emancipate his slaves, and that, if he did
not do this, it would, at any rate, make him more kind and humane. I
was disappointed in both these respects. It neither made him to be
humane to his slaves, nor to emancipate them. If it had any effect on
his character, it made him more cruel and hateful in all his ways; for I
believe him to have been a much worse man after his conversion than
before. Prior to his conversion, he relied upon his own depravity to
shield and sustain him in his savage barbarity; but after his conversion, he found religious sanction and support for his slaveholding cruelty. He made the greatest pretensions to piety. His house was the
house of prayer. He prayed morning, noon, and night. He very soon
distinguished himself among his brethren, and was soon made a class-
leader† and exhorter. His activity in revivals was great, and he proved
himself an instrument in the hands of the church in converting many
souls. His house was the preachers' home. They used to take great
pleasure in coming there to put up; for while he starved us, he stuffed
them. We have had three or four preachers there at a time. The names
of those who used to come most frequently while I lived there, were
Mr. Storks, Mr. Ewery, Mr. Humphry, and Mr. Hickey. I have also
seen Mr. George Cookman at our house. We slaves loved Mr. Cookman.[30] We believed him to be a good man. We thought him instru-
mental in getting Mr. Samuel Harrison, a very rich slaveholder, to
emancipate his slaves; and by some means got the impression that he
was laboring to effect the emancipation of all the slaves. When he was
at our house, we were sure to be called in to prayers. When the others were there, we were sometimes called in and sometimes not. Mr.
Cookman took more notice of us than either of the other ministers.
He could not come among us without betraying his sympathy for us,
and, stupid as we were, we had the sagacity to see it.

   While I lived with my master in St. Michael's, there was a white
young man, a Mr. Wilson, who proposed to keep a Sabbath school
for the instruction of such slaves as might be disposed to learn to read

---

*Religious service, usually held outdoors.
†Methodist congregations were divided into "classes" that met under a "class-leader."

the New Testament. We met but three times, when Mr. West and Mr. Fairbanks, both class-leaders, with many others, came upon us with sticks and other missiles, drove us off, and forbade us to meet again. Thus ended our little Sabbath school in the pious town of St. Michael's.

I have said my master found religious sanction for his cruelty. As an example, I will state one of many facts going to prove the charge. I have seen him tie up a lame young woman, and whip her with a heavy cowskin upon her naked shoulders, causing the warm red blood to drip; and, in justification of the bloody deed, he would quote this passage of Scripture—"He that knoweth his master's will, and doeth it not, shall be beaten with many stripes."*

Master would keep this lacerated young woman tied up in this horrid situation four or five hours at a time. I have known him to tie her up early in the morning, and whip her before breakfast; leave her, go to his store, return at dinner, and whip her again, cutting her in the places already made raw with his cruel lash. The secret of master's cruelty toward "Henny" is found in the fact of her being almost helpless. When quite a child, she fell into the fire, and burned herself horribly. Her hands were so burnt that she never got the use of them. She could do very little but bear heavy burdens. She was to master a bill of expense; and as he was a mean man, she was a constant offence to him. He seemed desirous of getting the poor girl out of existence. He gave her away once to his sister; but, being a poor gift, she was not disposed to keep her. Finally, my benevolent master, to use his own words, "set her adrift to take care of herself." Here was a recently-converted man, holding on upon the mother, and at the same time turning out her helpless child, to starve and die! Master Thomas was one of the many pious slaveholders who hold slaves for the very charitable purpose of taking care of them.

My master and myself had quite a number of differences. He found me unsuitable to his purpose. My city life, he said, had had a very pernicious effect upon me. It had almost ruined me for every good purpose, and fitted me for every thing which was bad. One of my greatest faults was that of letting his horse run away, and go down to his father-in-law's farm, which was about five miles from St.

---

*Reference to the Bible, Luke 12:47.

Michael's. I would then have to go after it. My reason for this kind
of carelessness, or carefulness, was, that I could always get something
to eat when I went there. Master William Hamilton, my master's
father-in-law, always gave his slaves enough to eat. I never left there
hungry, no matter how great the need of my speedy return. Master
Thomas at length said he would stand it no longer. I had lived with
him nine months, during which time he had given me a number of
severe whippings, all to no good purpose. He resolved to put me out,
as he said, to be broken; and, for this purpose, he let me for one year
to a man named Edward Covey. Mr. Covey was a poor man, a farm-
renter. He rented the place upon which he lived, as also the hands
with which he tilled it. Mr. Covey had acquired a very high reputation for breaking young slaves, and this reputation was of immense
value to him. It enabled him to get his farm tilled with much less expense to himself than he could have had it done without such a reputation. Some slaveholders thought it not much loss to allow Mr.
Covey to have their slaves one year, for the sake of the training to
which they were subjected, without any other compensation. He
could hire young help with great ease, in consequence of this reputation. Added to the natural good qualities of Mr. Covey, he was a professor of religion—a pious soul—a member and a class-leader in the
Methodist church. All of this added weight to his reputation as a
"nigger-breaker." I was aware of all the facts, having been made acquainted with them by a young man who had lived there. I nevertheless made the change gladly; for I was sure of getting enough to
eat, which is not the smallest consideration to a hungry man.

CHAPTER X

I LEFT MASTER THOMAS'S house, and went to live with Mr. Covey, on the 1st of January, 1833.* I was now, for the first time in my life, a field hand. In my new employment, I found myself even more awkward than a country boy appeared to be in a large city. I had been at my new home but one week before Mr. Covey gave me a very severe whipping, cutting my back, causing the blood to run, and raising ridges on my flesh as large as my little finger. The details of this affair are as follows: Mr. Covey sent me, very early in the morning of one of our coldest days in the month of January, to the woods, to get a load of wood. He gave me a team of unbroken oxen. He told me which was the in-hand ox, and which the off-hand one.† He then tied the end of a large rope around the horns of the in-hand ox, and gave me the other end of it, and told me, if the oxen started to run, that I must hold on upon the rope. I had never driven oxen before, and of course I was very awkward. I, however, succeeded in getting to the edge of the woods with little difficulty; but I had got a very few rods into the woods, when the oxen took fright, and started full tilt, carrying the cart against trees, and over stumps, in the most frightful manner. I expected every moment that my brains would be dashed out against the trees. After running thus for a considerable distance, they finally upset the cart, dashing it with great force against a tree, and threw themselves into a dense thicket. How I escaped death, I do not know. There I was, entirely alone, in a thick wood, in a place new to me. My cart was upset and shattered, my oxen were entangled among the young trees, and there was none to help me. After a long spell of effort, I succeeded in getting my cart righted, my oxen disentangled, and again yoked to the cart. I now proceeded with my team to the place where I had, the day before,

---

*Actually it was January 1834, when Douglass was sixteen years old.
†In a pair of oxen hitched to a wagon, the "in-hand" ox is on the left and the "off-hand" ox is on the right.

been chopping wood, and loaded my cart pretty heavily, thinking in this way to tame my oxen. I then proceeded on my way home. I had now consumed one half of the day. I got out of the woods safely, and now felt out of danger. I stopped my oxen to open the woods gate; and just as I did so, before I could get hold of my ox-rope, the oxen again started, rushed through the gate, catching it between the wheel and the body of the cart, tearing it to pieces, and coming within a few inches of crushing me against the gate-post. Thus twice, in one short day, I escaped death by the merest chance. On my return, I told Mr. Covey what had happened, and how it happened. He ordered me to return to the woods again immediately. I did so, and he followed on after me. Just as I got into the woods, he came up and told me to stop my cart, and that he would teach me how to trifle away my time, and break gates. He then went to a large gum-tree, and with his axe cut three large switches, and, after trimming them up neatly with his pocket-knife, he ordered me to take off my clothes. I made him no answer, but stood with my clothes on. He repeated his order. I still made him no answer, nor did I move to strip myself. Upon this he rushed at me with the fierceness of a tiger, tore off my clothes, and lashed me till he had worn out his switches, cutting me so savagely as to leave the marks visible for a long time after. This whipping was the first of a number just like it, and for similar offences.

I lived with Mr. Covey one year. During the first six months, of that year, scarce a week passed without his whipping me. I was seldom free from a sore back. My awkwardness was almost always his excuse for whipping me. We were worked fully up to the point of endurance. Long before day we were up, our horses fed, and by the first approach of day we were off to the field with our hoes and ploughing teams. Mr. Covey gave us enough to eat, but scarce time to eat it. We were often less than five minutes taking our meals. We were often in the field from the first approach of day till its last lingering ray had left us; and at saving-fodder time,* midnight often caught us in the field binding blades.

Covey would be out with us. The way he used to stand it, was this. He would spend the most of his afternoons in bed. He would then come out fresh in the evening, ready to urge us on with his words, ex-

---

*The harvesting of the crops.

ample, and frequently with the whip. Mr. Covey was one of the few slaveholders who could and did work with his hands. He was a hard-working man. He knew by himself just what a man or a boy could do. There was no deceiving him. His work went on in his absence al-most as well as in his presence; and he had the faculty of making us feel that he was ever present with us. This he did by surprising us. He seldom approached the spot where we were at work openly, if he could do it secretly. He always aimed at taking us by surprise. Such was his cunning, that we used to call him, among ourselves, "the snake."* When we were at work in the cornfield, he would sometimes crawl on his hands and knees to avoid detection, and all at once he would rise nearly in our midst, and scream out, "Ha, ha! Come, come! Dash on, dash on!" This being his mode of attack, it was never safe to stop a single minute. His comings were like a thief in the night. He appeared to us as being ever at hand. He was under every tree, behind every stump, in every bush, and at every window, on the plan-tation. He would sometimes mount his horse, as if bound to St. Michael's, a distance of seven miles, and in half an hour afterwards you would see him coiled up in the corner of the wood-fence, watch-ing every motion of the slaves. He would, for this purpose, leave his horse tied up in the woods. Again, he would sometimes walk up to us, and give us orders as though he was upon the point of starting on a long journey, turn his back upon us, and make as though he was going to the house to get ready; and, before he would get half way thither, he would turn short and crawl into a fence-corner, or behind some tree, and there watch us till the going down of the sun.

Mr. Covey's *forte* consisted in his power to deceive. His life was devoted to planning and perpetrating the grossest deceptions. Every thing he possessed in the shape of learning or religion, he made con-form to his disposition to deceive. He seemed to think himself equal to deceiving the Almighty. He would make a short prayer in the morning, and a long prayer at night; and, strange as it may seem, few men would at times appear more devotional than he. The exercises of his family devotions were always commenced with singing; and, as he was a very poor singer himself, the duty of raising the hymn gener-

---

*In the context of Covey's ruthless trickery and treachery, this nickname gives the story a mythical, evil twist.

ally came upon me. He would read his hymn, and nod at me to com-
mence. I would at times do so; at others, I would not.* My non-
compliance would almost always produce much confusion. To show
himself independent of me, he would start and stagger through with
his hymn in the most discordant manner. In this state of mind, he
prayed with more than ordinary spirit. Poor man! such was his disposition, and success at deceiving, I do verily believe that he sometimes deceived himself into the solemn belief, that he was a sincere
worshipper of the most high God; and this, too, at a time when he
may be said to have been guilty of compelling his woman slave to
commit the sin of adultery. The facts in the case are these: Mr. Covey
was a poor man; he was just commencing in life; he was only able to
buy one slave; and, shocking as is the fact, he bought her, as he said,
for a *breeder* This woman was named Caroline. Mr. Covey bought her
from Mr. Thomas Lowe, about six miles from St. Michael's. She was
a large, able-bodied woman, about twenty years old. She had already
given birth to one child, which proved her to be just what he wanted.
After buying her, he hired a married man of Mr. Samuel Harrison,
to live with him one year; and him he used to fasten up with her
every night! The result was, that, at the end of the year, the miserable
woman gave birth to twins. At this result Mr. Covey seemed to be
highly pleased, both with the man and the wretched woman. Such
was his joy, and that of his wife, that nothing they could do for Caroline during her confinement was too good, or too hard, to be done.
The children were regarded as being quite an addition to his wealth.

If at any one time of my life more than another, I was made to
drink the bitterest dregs of slavery, that time was during the first six
months of my stay with Mr. Covey. We were worked in all weathers.
It was never too hot or too cold; it could never rain, blow, hail, or
snow, too hard for us to work in the field. Work, work, work, was
scarcely more the order of the day than of the night. The longest
days were too short for him, and the shortest nights too long for
him. I was somewhat unmanageable when I first went there, but a
few months of this discipline tamed me. Mr. Covey succeeded in
breaking me. I was broken in body, soul, and spirit. My natural elas-

*"How can we sing the Lord's song in a foreign land?" (see the Bible, Psalm 137:4,
New American Standard version).

ticity was crushed, my intellect languished, the disposition to read departed, the cheerful spark that lingered about my eye died; the dark night of slavery closed in upon me; and behold a man transformed into a brute!

Sunday was my only leisure time. I spent this in a sort of beastlike stupor, between sleep and wake, under some large tree. At times I would rise up, a flash of energetic freedom would dart through, my soul, accompanied with a faint beam of hope, that flickered for a moment, and then vanished. I sank down again, mourning over my wretched condition. I was sometimes prompted to take my life, and that of Covey, but was prevented by a combination of hope and fear. My sufferings on this plantation seem now like a dream rather than a stern reality.

Our house stood within a few rods of the Chesapeake Bay, whose broad bosom was ever white with sails from every quarter of the habitable globe. Those beautiful vessels, robed in purest white, so delightful to the eye of freemen, were to me so many shrouded ghosts, to terrify and torment me with thoughts of my wretched condition. I have often, in the deep stillness of a summer's Sabbath, stood all alone upon the lofty banks of that noble bay, and traced, with saddened heart and tearful eye, the countless number of sails moving off to the mighty ocean. The sight of these always affected me powerfully. My thoughts would compel utterance; and there, with no audience but the Almighty, I would pour out my soul's complaint, in my rude way, with an apostrophe to the moving multitude of ships:—

"You are loosed from your moorings,* and are free; I am fast in my chains, and am a slave! You move merrily before the gentle gale, and I sadly before the bloody whip! You are freedom's swift-winged angels, that fly round the world; I am confined in bands of iron! O that I were free! O, that I were on one of your gallant decks, and under your protecting wing! Alas! betwixt me and you, the turbid waters roll. Go on, go on. O that I could also go! Could I but swim! If I could fly! O, why was I born a man, of whom to make a brute! The glad ship is gone; she hides in the dim distance. I am left in the hottest hell of unending slavery. O God, save me! God, deliver me! Let me be free! Is there any God? Why am I a slave? I will run away.

---

*Released from confining anchors and chains.

I will not stand it. Get caught, or get clear, I'll try it. I had as well die with ague* as the fever. I have only one life to lose. I had as well be killed running as die standing. Only think of it; one hundred miles straight north, and I am free! Try it? Yes! God helping me, I will. It cannot be that I shall live and die a slave. I will take to the water. This very bay shall bear me into freedom. The steamboats steered in a north-east course from North Point. I will do the same; and when I get to the head of the bay, I will turn my canoe adrift, and walk straight through Delaware into Pennsylvania. When I get there, I shall not be required to have a pass; I can travel without being disturbed. Let but the first opportunity offer, and, come what will, I am off. Meanwhile, I will try to bear up under the yoke. I am not the only slave in the world. Why should I fret? I can bear as much as any of them. Besides, I am but a boy, and all boys are bound to some one. It may be that my misery in slavery will only increase my happiness when I get free. There is a better day coming."[31]

Thus I used to think, and thus I used to speak to myself; goaded almost to madness at one moment, and at the next reconciling myself to my wretched lot.

I have already intimated that my condition was much worse, during the first six months of my stay at Mr. Covey's, than in the last six. The circumstances leading to the change in Mr. Covey's course toward me form an epoch in my humble history. You have seen how a man was made a slave; you shall see how a slave was made a man. On one of the hottest days of the month of August, 1833, Bill Smith, William Hughes, a slave named Eli, and myself, were engaged in fanning wheat.† Hughes was clearing the fanned wheat from before the fan, Eli was turning, Smith was feeding, and I was carrying wheat to the fan. The work was simple, requiring strength rather than intellect; yet, to one entirely unused to such work, it came very hard. About three o'clock of that day, I broke down; my strength failed me; I was seized with a violent aching of the head, attended with extreme dizziness; I trembled in every limb. Finding what was coming, I nerved myself up, feeling it would never do to stop work. I stood as

---

*Fever (as with malaria) characterized by periods of chills and sweating that come and go.

†Using a machine to separate the wheat from the worthless husk, called chaff.

long as I could stagger to the hopper with grain. When I could stand no longer, I fell, and felt as if held down by an immense weight. The fan of course stopped; every one had his own work to do; and no one could do the work of the other, and have his own go on at the same time.

Mr. Covey was at the house, about one hundred yards from the treading-yard where we were fanning. On hearing the fan stop, he left immediately, and came to the spot where we were. He hastily inquired what the matter was. Bill answered that I was sick, and there was no one to bring wheat to the fan. I had by this time crawled away under the side of the post and rail-fence by which the yard was enclosed, hoping to find relief by getting out of the sun. He then asked where I was. He was told by one of the hands. He came to the spot, and, after looking at me awhile, asked me what was the matter. I told him as well as I could, for I scarce had strength to speak. He then gave me a savage kick in the side, and told me to get up. I tried to do so, but fell back in the attempt. He gave me another kick, and again told me to rise. I again tried, and succeeded in gaining my feet; but, stooping to get the tub with which I was feeding the fan, I again staggered and fell. While down in this situation, Mr. Covey took up the hickory slat* with which Hughes had been striking off the half-bushel measure, and with it gave me a heavy blow upon the head, making a large wound, and the blood ran freely; and with this again told me to get up. I made no effort to comply, having now made up my mind to let him do his worst. In a short time after receiving this blow, my head grew better. Mr. Covey had now left me to my fate. At this moment I resolved, for the first time, to go to my master, enter a complaint, and ask his protection. In order to [do] this, I must that afternoon walk seven miles; and this, under the circumstances, was truly a severe undertaking. I was exceedingly feeble; made so as much by the kicks and blows which I received, as by the severe fit of sickness to which I had been subjected. I, however, watched my chance, while Covey was looking in an opposite direction, and started for St. Michael's. I succeeded in getting a considerable distance on my way to the woods, when Covey discovered me, and

---

*Wooden board.

called after me to come back, threatening what he would do if I did not come. I disregarded both his calls and his threats, and made my way to the woods as fast as my feeble state would allow; and thinking I might be overhauled* by him if I kept the road, I walked through the woods, keeping far enough from the road to avoid detection, and near enough to prevent losing my way. I had not gone far before my little strength again failed me. I could go no farther. I fell down, and lay for a considerable time. The blood was yet oozing from the wound on my head. For a time I thought I should bleed to death; and think now that I should have done so, but that the blood so matted my hair as to stop the wound. After lying there about three quarters of an hour, I nerved myself up again, and started on my way, through bogs and briers, barefooted and bareheaded, tearing my feet sometimes at nearly every step; and after a journey of about seven miles, occupying some five hours to perform it, I arrived at master's store. I then presented an appearance enough to affect any but a heart of iron. From the crown of my head to my feet, I was covered with blood. My hair was all clotted with dust and blood; my shirt was stiff with blood. My legs and feet were torn in sundry places with briers and thorns, and were also covered with blood. I suppose I looked like a man who had escaped a den of wild beasts, and barely escaped them. In this state I appeared before my master, humbly entreating him to interpose his authority for my protection. I told him all the circumstances as well as I could, and it seemed, as I spoke, at times to affect him. He would then walk the floor, and seek to justify Covey by saying he expected I deserved it. He asked me what I wanted. I told him, to let me get a new home; that as sure as I lived with Mr. Covey again, I should live with but to die with him; that Covey would surely kill me; he was in a fair way for it. Master Thomas ridiculed the idea that there was any danger of Mr. Covey's killing me, and said that he knew Mr. Covey; that he was a good man, and that he could not think of taking me from him; that, should he do so, he would lose the whole year's wages; that I belonged to Mr. Covey for one year, and that I must go back to him, come what might; and that I must not trouble him with any more stories, or that he would himself *get hold of me*. After threatening me thus, he gave me a very

---

*Overtaken.

large dose of salts, telling me that I might remain in St. Michael's that night, (it being quite late,) but that I must be off back to Mr. Covey's early in the morning; and that if I did not, he would *get hold of me*, which meant that he would whip me. I remained all night, and, according to his orders, I started off to Covey's in the morning, (Saturday morning,) wearied in body and broken in spirit. I got no supper that night, or breakfast that morning. I reached Covey's about nine o'clock; and just as I was getting over the fence that divided Mrs. Kemp's fields from ours, out ran Covey with his cowskin, to give me another whipping. Before he could reach me, I succeeded in getting to the cornfield; and as the corn was very high, it afforded me the means of hiding. He seemed very angry, and searched for me a long time. My behavior was altogether unaccountable. He finally gave up the chase, thinking, I suppose, that I must come home for something to eat; he would give himself no further trouble in looking for me. I spent that day mostly in the woods, having the alternative before me,—to go home and be whipped to death, or stay in the woods and be starved to death. That night, I fell in with Sandy Jenkins,* a slave with whom I was somewhat acquainted. Sandy had a free wife† who lived about four miles from Mr. Covey's; and it being Saturday, he was on his way to see her. I told him my circumstances, and he very kindly invited me to go home with him. I went home with him, and talked this whole matter over, and got his advice as to what course it was best for me to pursue. I found Sandy an old adviser.[32] He told me, with great solemnity, I must go back to Covey; but that before I went, I must go with him into another part of the woods, where there was a certain *root*, which, if I would take some of it with me, carrying it *always on my right side*, would render it impossible for Mr. Covey, or any other white man, to whip me. He said he had carried it for years; and since he had done so, he had never received a blow, and never expected to while he carried it. I at first rejected the idea, that the simple carrying of a root in my pocket would have any such effect as he had said, and was not disposed to take it; but Sandy impressed the necessity with much earnestness, telling me it could do

---

*Property of William Groome, a merchant in Easton, Maryland; Jenkins was hired out to Mrs. Covey's father, Mr. Caulk.

†That is, she was not legally a slave; further, she owned her own cabin.

no harm, if it did no good. To please him, I at length took the root, and, according to his direction, carried it upon my right side. This was Sunday morning. I immediately started for home; and upon entering the yard gate, out came Mr. Covey on his way to meeting. He spoke to me very kindly, bade me drive the pigs from a lot near by, and passed on towards the church. Now, this singular conduct of Mr. Covey really made me begin to think that there was something in the *root* which Sandy had given me; and had it been on any other day than Sunday, I could have attributed the conduct to no other cause than the influence of that root; and as it was, I was half inclined to think the *root* to be something more than I at first had taken it to be. All went well till Monday morning. On this morning, the virtue of the *root* was fully tested. Long before daylight, I was called to go and rub, curry, and feed, the horses. I obeyed, and was glad to obey. But whilst thus engaged, whilst in the act of throwing down some blades from the loft, Mr. Covey entered the stable with a long rope; and just as I was half out of the loft, he caught hold of my legs, and was about tying me. As soon as I found what he was up to, I gave a sudden spring, and as I did so, he holding to my legs, I was brought sprawling on the stable floor. Mr. Covey seemed now to think he had me, and could do what he pleased; but at this moment—from whence came the spirit I don't know—I resolved to fight; and, suiting my action to the resolution, I seized Covey hard by the throat; and as I did so, I rose. He held on to me, and I to him. My resistance was so entirely unexpected, that Covey seemed taken all aback. He trembled like a leaf. This gave me assurance, and I held him uneasy, causing the blood to run where I touched him with the ends of my fingers. Mr. Covey soon called out to Hughes for help. Hughes came, and, while Covey held me, attempted to tie my right hand. While he was in the act of doing so, I watched my chance, and gave him a heavy kick close under the ribs. This kick fairly sickened Hughes, so that he left me in the hands of Mr. Covey. This kick had the effect of not only weakening Hughes, but Covey also. When he saw Hughes bending over with pain, his courage quailed. He asked me if I meant to persist in my resistance. I told him I did, come what might; that he had used me like a brute for six months, and that I was determined to be used so no longer. With that, he strove to drag me to a stick that was lying just out of the stable door. He meant to knock me down. But just as he was leaning over to get the stick, I seized him with both hands by his collar, and brought him by a sudden snatch to the ground. By this time, Bill came. Covey called upon him for assistance. Bill wanted to know what he could do. Covey said, "Take hold of him, take hold of him!" Bill said his master hired him out to work, and not to help to whip me; so he left Covey and myself to fight our own battle out. We were at it for nearly two hours. Covey at length let me go, puffing and blowing at a great rate, saying that if I had not resisted, he would not have whipped me at all. I considered him as getting entirely the worst end of the bargain; for he had drawn no blood from me, but I had from him. The whole six months afterwards, that I spent with Mr. Covey, he never laid the weight of his finger upon me in anger. He would occasionally say, he didn't want to get hold of me again. "No," thought I, "you need not; for you will come off worse than you did before."

This battle with Mr. Covey was the turning-point in my career as a slave. It rekindled the few expiring embers of freedom, and revived within me a sense of my own manhood. It recalled the departed self-confidence, and inspired me again with a determination to be free. The gratification afforded by the triumph was a full compensation for whatever else might follow, even death itself. He only can understand the deep satisfaction which I experienced, who has himself repelled by force the bloody arm of slavery. I felt as I never felt before. It was a glorious resurrection, from the tomb of slavery, to the heaven of freedom. My long-crushed spirit rose, cowardice departed, bold defiance took its place; and I now resolved that, however long I might remain a slave in form, the day had passed forever when I could be a slave in fact. I did not hesitate to let it be known of me, that the white man who expected to succeed in whipping, must also succeed in killing me.

From this time I was never again what might be called fairly whipped,* though I remained a slave four years afterwards. I had several fights, but was never whipped.

It was for a long time a matter of surprise to me why Mr. Covey did not immediately have me taken by the constable to the whipping-post, and there regularly whipped for the crime of raising my

*Openly whipped, without interruption or protest.

hand against a white man in defence of myself. And the only explanation I can now think of does not entirely satisfy me; but such as it
is, I will give it. Mr. Covey enjoyed the most unbounded reputation
for being a first-rate overseer and negro-breaker. It was of considerable importance to him. That reputation was at stake; and had he
sent me—a boy about sixteen years old—to the public whipping-
post, his reputation would have been lost; so, to save his reputation,
he suffered me to go unpunished.

My term of actual service to Mr. Edward Covey ended on Christmas day, 1833. The days between Christmas and New Year's day are
allowed as holidays; and, accordingly, we were not required to perform any labor, more than to feed and take care of the stock. This
time we regarded as our own, by the grace of our masters; and we
therefore used or abused it nearly as we pleased. Those of us who had
families at a distance, were generally allowed to spend the whole six
days in their society. This time, however, was spent in various ways.
The staid, sober, thinking, and industrious ones of our number would
employ themselves in making cornbrooms,* mats, horse-collars, and
baskets; and another class of us would spend the time in hunting
opossums, hares, and coons. But by far the larger part engaged in
such sports and merriments as playing ball, wrestling, running foot-
races, fiddling, dancing, and drinking whisky; and this latter mode of
spending the time was by far the most agreeable to the feelings of our
masters. A slave who would work during the holidays was considered
by our masters as scarcely deserving them. He was regarded as one
who rejected the favor of his master. It was deemed a disgrace not to
get drunk at Christmas; and he was regarded as lazy indeed, who had
not provided himself with the necessary means, during the yeat, to
get whisky enough to last him through Christmas.

From what I know of the effect of these holidays upon the slave,
I believe them to be among the most effective means in the hands of
the slaveholder in keeping down the spirit of insurrection. Were the
slaveholders at once to abandon this practice, I have not the slightest
doubt it would lead to an immediate insurrection among the slaves.
These holidays serve as conductors, or safety-valves, to carry off the
rebellious spirit of enslaved humanity. But for these, the slave would

---

*Brooms made from the long stems of corn plants.

be forced up to the wildest desperation; and woe betide the slave-holder, the day he ventures to remove or hinder the operation of those conductors! I warn him that, in such an event, a spirit will go forth in their midst, more to be dreaded than the most appalling earthquake.

The holidays are part and parcel of the gross fraud, wrong, and in-humanity of slavery. They are professedly a custom established by the benevolence of the slaveholders; but I undertake to say, it is the result of selfishness, and one of the grossest frauds committed upon the down-trodden slave. They do not give the slaves this time because they would not like to have their work during its continuance, but because they know it would be unsafe to deprive them of it. This will be seen by the fact, that the slaveholders like to have their slaves spend those days just in such a manner as to make them as glad of their ending as of their beginning. Their object seems to be, to dis-gust their slaves with freedom, by plunging them into the lowest depths of dissipation. For instance, the slaveholders not only like to see the slave drink of his own accord, but will adopt various plans to make him drunk. One plan is, to make bets on their slaves, as to who can drink the most whisky without getting drunk; and in this way they succeed in getting whole multitudes to drink to excess. Thus, when the slave asks for virtuous freedom, the cunning slaveholder, knowing his ignorance, cheats him with a dose of vicious dissipation, artfully labelled with the name of liberty. The most of us used to drink it down, and the result was just what might be supposed: Many of us were led to think that there was little to choose between liberty and slavery. We felt, and very properly too, that we had. almost as well be slaves to man as to rum. So, when the holidays ended, we staggered up from the filth of our wallowing, took a long breath, and marched to the field,—feeling, upon the whole, rather glad to go, from what our master had deceived us into a belief was freedom, back to the arms of slavery.[33]

I have said that this mode of treatment is a part of the whole sys-tem of fraud and inhumanity of slavery It is so. The mode here adopted to disgust the slave with freedom, by allowing him to see only the abuse of it, is carried out in other things. For instance, a slave loves molasses; he steals some. His master, in many cases, goes off to town, and buys a large quantity; he returns, takes his whip, and commands the slave to eat the molasses, until the poor fellow is made sick at the very mention of it. The same mode is sometimes adopted to make the slaves refrain from asking for more food than their regular allowance. A slave runs through his allowance, and applies for more. His master is enraged at him; but, not willing to send him off without food, gives him more than is necessary, and compels him to eat it within a given time. Then, if he complains that he cannot eat it, he is said to be satisfied neither full nor fasting, and is whipped for being hard to please! I have an abundance of such illustrations of the same principle, drawn from my own observation, but think the cases I have cited sufficient. The practice is a very common one.

On the first of January, 1834, I left Mr. Covey, and went to live with Mr. William Freeland, who lived about three miles from St. Michael's. I soon found Mr. Freeland a very different man from Mr. Covey. Though not rich, he was what would be called an educated southern gentleman. Mr. Covey, as I have shown, was a well-trained negro-breaker and slave-driver. The former (slaveholder though he was) seemed to possess some regard for honor, some reverence for justice, and some respect for humanity. The latter seemed totally insensible to all such sentiments. Mr. Freeland had many of the faults peculiar to slaveholders, such as being very passionate and fretful; but I must do him the justice to say, that he was exceedingly free from those degrading vices to which Mr. Covey was constantly addicted. The one was open and frank, and we always knew where to find him. The other was a most artful deceiver, and could be understood only by such as were skillful enough to detect his cunningly-devised frauds. Another advantage I gained in my new master was, he made no pretensions to, or profession of, religion; and this, in my opinion, was truly a great advantage. I assert most unhesitatingly, that the religion of the south is a mere covering for the most horrid crimes,—a justifier of the most appalling barbarity,—a sanctifier of the most hateful frauds,—and a dark shelter under which the darkest, foulest, grossest, and most infernal deeds of slaveholders find the strongest protection. Were I to be again reduced to the chains of slavery, next to that enslavement, I should regard being the slave of a religious master the greatest calamity that could befall me. For of all slaveholders with whom I have ever met, religious slaveholders are the worst. I have ever found them the meanest and basest, the most cruel

and cowardly, of all others. It was my unhappy lot not only to belong
to a religious slaveholder, but to live in a community of such reli-
gionists. Very near Mr. Freeland lived the Rev. Daniel Weeden, and
in the same neighborhood lived the Rev. Rigby Hopkins. These were
members and ministers in the Reformed Methodist Church. Mr.
Weeden owned, among others, a woman slave, whose name I have
forgotten. This woman's back, for weeks, was kept literally raw, made
so by the lash of this merciless, *religious* wretch. He used to hire
hands. His maxim was, Behave well or behave ill, it is the duty of a
master occasionally to whip a slave, to remind him of his master's authority. Such was his theory, and such his practice.

Mr. Hopkins was even worse than Mr. Weeden. His chief boast
was his ability to manage slaves. The peculiar feature of his government was that of whipping slaves in advance of deserving it. He always managed to have one or more of his slaves to whip every
Monday morning. He did this to alarm their fears, and strike terror
into those who escaped. His plan was to whip for the smallest offences, to prevent the commission of large ones. Mr. Hopkins could
always find some excuse for whipping a slave. It would astonish one,
unaccustomed to a slaveholding life, to see with what wonderful ease
a slaveholder can find things, of which to make occasion to whip a
slave. A mere look, word, or motion,—a mistake, accident, or want
of power,—are all matters for which a slave may be whipped at any
time. Does a slave look dissatisfied? It is said, he has the devil in him,
and it must be whipped out. Does he speak loudly when spoken to
by his master? Then he is getting high-minded, and should be taken
down a button-hole lower. Does he forget to pull off his hat at the
approach of a white person? Then he is wanting in reverence, and
should be whipped for it. Does he ever venture to vindicate his conduct, when censured for it? Then he is guilty of impudence,—one of
the greatest crimes of which a slave can be guilty. Does he ever venture to suggest a different mode of doing things from that pointed
out by his master? He is indeed presumptuous, and getting above
himself; and nothing less than a flogging will do for him. Does he,
while ploughing, break a plough,—or, while hoeing, break a hoe? It
is owing to his carelessness, and for it a slave must always be
whipped. Mr. Hopkins could always find something of this sort to
justify the use of the lash, and he seldom failed to embrace such op-

portunities. There was not a man in the whole county, with whom
the slaves who had the getting their own home, would not prefer to
live, rather than with this Rev. Mr. Hopkins. And yet there was not
a man any where round, who made higher professions of religion, or
was more active in revivals,—more attentive to the class, love-feast,
prayer and preaching meetings, or more devotional in his family,—
that prayed earlier, later, louder, and longer,—than this same rev-
erend slave-driver, Rigby Hopkins.

But to return to Mr. Freeland, and to my experience while in his
employment. He, like Mr. Covey, gave us enough to eat; but, unlike
Mr. Covey, he also gave us sufficient time to take our meals. He
worked us hard, but always between sunrise and sunset. He required
a good deal of work to be done, but gave us good tools with which to
work. His farm was large, but he employed hands enough to work it,
and with ease, compared with many of his neighbors. My treatment,
while in his employment, was heavenly, compared with what I experienced at the hands of Mr. Edward Covey.

Mr. Freeland was himself the owner of but two slaves. Their
names were Henry Harris and John Harris. The rest of his hands he
hired. These consisted of myself, Sandy Jenkins,* and Handy Cald-
well. Henry and John were quite intelligent, and in a very little while
after I went there, I succeeded in creating in them a strong desire to
learn how to read. This desire soon sprang up in the others also. They
very soon mustered up some old spelling-books, and nothing would
do but that I must keep a Sabbath school. I agreed to do so, and accordingly devoted my Sundays to teaching these my loved fellow-
slaves how to read. Neither of them knew his letters when I went
there. Some of the slaves of the neighboring farms found what was
going on, and also availed themselves of this little opportunity to
learn to read. It was understood, among all who came, that there
must be as little display about it as possible. It was necessary to keep
our religious masters at St. Michael's unacquainted with the fact,
that, instead of spending the Sabbath in wrestling, boxing, and

*Author's note: This is the same man who gave me the roots to prevent my being
whipped by Mr. Covey. He was "a clever soul." We used frequently to talk about the
fight with Covey, and as often as we did so, he would claim my success as the result
of the roots which he gave me. This superstition is very common among the more ignorant slaves. A slave seldom dies but that his death is attributed to trickery.

drinking whisky, we were trying to learn how to read the will of God; for they had much rather see us engaged in those degrading sports, than to see us behaving like intellectual, moral, and accountable beings. My blood boils as I think of the bloody manner in which Messrs. Wright Fairbanks and Garrison West, both class-leaders, in connection with many others, rushed in upon us with sticks and stones, and broke up our virtuous little Sabbath school, at St. Michael's—all calling themselves Christians! humble followers of the Lord Jesus Christ! But I am again digressing.

I held my Sabbath school at the house of a free colored man, whose name I deem it imprudent to mention; for should it be known, it might embarrass him greatly, though the crime of holding the school was committed ten years ago. I had at one time over forty scholars, and those of the right sort, ardently desiring to learn. They were of all ages, though mostly men and women. I look back to those Sundays with an amount of pleasure not to be expressed. They were great days to my soul. The work of instructing my dear fellow-slaves was the sweetest engagement with which I was ever blessed. We loved each other, and to leave them at the close of the Sabbath was a severe cross indeed. When I think that these precious souls are to-day shut up in the prison-house of slavery, my feelings overcome me, and I am almost ready to ask, "Does a righteous God govern the universe? and for what does he hold the thunders in his right hand, if not to smite the oppressor, and deliver the spoiled out of the hand of the spoiler?" These dear souls came not to Sabbath school because it was popular to do so, nor did I teach them because it was reputable to be thus engaged. Every moment they spent in that school, they were liable to be taken up, and given thirty-nine lashes. They came because they wished to learn. Their minds had been starved by their cruel masters. They had been shut up in mental darkness. I taught them, because it was the delight of my soul to be doing something that looked like bettering the condition of my race. I kept up my school nearly the whole year I lived with Mr. Freeland; and, beside my Sabbath school, I devoted three evenings in the week, during the winter, to teaching the slaves at home. And I have the happiness to know, that several of those who came to Sabbath school learned how to read; and that one, at least, is now free through my agency.

The year passed off smoothly. It seemed only about half as long as the year which preceded it. I went through it without receiving a single blow. I will give Mr. Freeland the credit of being the best master I ever had, *till I became my own master*. For the ease with which I passed the year, I was, however, somewhat indebted to the society of my fellow-slaves. They were noble souls; they not only possessed loving hearts, but brave ones. We were linked and interlinked with each other. I loved them with a love stronger than any thing I have experienced since. It is sometimes said that we slaves do not love and confide in each other. In answer to this assertion, I can say, I never loved any or confided in any people more than my fellow-slaves, and especially those with whom I lived at Mr. Freeland's. I believe we would have died for each other. We never undertook to do any thing, of any importance, without a mutual consultation. We never moved separately. We were one; and as much so by our tempers and dispositions, as by the mutual hardships to which we were necessarily subjected by our condition as slaves.

At the close of the year 1834, Mr. Freeland again hired me of my master, for the year 1835. But, by this time, I began to want to live *upon free land* as well as *with Freeland*; and I was no longer content, therefore, to live with him or any other slaveholder. I began, with the commencement of the year, to prepare myself for a final struggle, which should decide my fate one way or the other. My tendency was upward. I was fast approaching manhood, and year after year had passed, and I was still a slave. These thoughts roused me—I must do something. I therefore resolved that 1835 should not pass without witnessing an attempt, on my part, to secure my liberty. But I was not willing to cherish this determination alone. My fellow-slaves were dear to me. I was anxious to have them participate with me in this, my life-giving determination. I therefore, though with great prudence, commenced early to ascertain their views and feelings in regard to their condition, and to imbue their minds with thoughts of freedom. I bent myself to devising ways and means for our escape, and meanwhile strove, on all fitting occasions, to impress them with the gross fraud and inhumanity of slavery. I went first to Henry, next to John, then to the others. I found, in them all, warm hearts and noble spirits. They were ready to hear, and ready to act when a feasible plan should be proposed. This was what I wanted. I talked to them of our want of manhood, if we submitted to our enslavement

without at least one noble effort to be free. We met often, and consulted frequently, and told our hopes and fears, recounted the difficulties, real and imagined, which we should be called on to meet. At
times we were almost disposed to give up, and try to content ourselves with our wretched lot; at others, we were firm and unbending
in our determination to go. Whenever we suggested any plan, there
was shrinking—the odds were fearful. Our path was beset with the
greatest obstacles; and if we succeeded in gaining the end of it, our
right to be free was yet questionable—we were yet liable to be returned to bondage. We could see no spot, this side of the ocean,
where we could be free. We knew nothing about Canada. Our
knowledge of the north did not extend farther than New York; and
to go there, and be forever harassed with the frightful liability of
being returned to slavery—with the certainty of being treated tenfold
worse than before—the thought was truly a horrible one, and one
which it was not easy to overcome. The case sometimes stood thus:
At every gate through which we were to pass, we saw a watchman—
at every ferry a guard—on every bridge a sentinel—and in every
wood a patrol. We were hemmed in upon every side. Here were the
difficulties, real or imagined—the good to be sought, and the evil to
be shunned. On the one hand, there stood slavery, a stern reality,
glaring frightfully upon us,—its robes already crimsoned with the
blood of millions, and even now feasting itself greedily upon our own
flesh. On the other hand, away back in the dim distance, under the
flickering light of the north star, behind some craggy hill or snow-
covered mountain, stood a doubtful freedom—half frozen—beckon-
ing us to come and share its hospitality. This in itself was sometimes
enough to stagger us; but when we permitted ourselves to survey the
road, we were frequently appalled. Upon either side we saw grim
death, assuming the most horrid shapes. Now it was starvation, causing us to eat our own flesh;—now we were contending with the
waves, and were drowned;—now we were overtaken, and torn to
pieces by the fangs of the terrible bloodhound. We were stung by
scorpions, chased by wild beasts, bitten by snakes, and finally, after
having nearly reached the desired spot,—after swimming rivers, en-
countering wild beasts, sleeping in the woods, suffering hunger and
nakedness,—we were overtaken by our pursuers, and, in our resis-

tance, we were shot dead upon the spot! I say, this picture sometimes appalled us, and made us

rather bear those ills we had,
Than fly to others, that we knew not of.*

In coming to a fixed determination to run away, we did more than Patrick Henry, when he resolved upon liberty or death. With us it was a doubtful liberty at most, and almost certain death if we failed. For my part, I should prefer death to hopeless bondage.

Sandy, one of our number, gave up the notion, but still encouraged us. Our company then consisted of Henry Harris, John Harris, Henry Bailey, Charles Roberts, and myself. Henry Bailey was my uncle, and belonged to my master. Charles married my aunt: he belonged to my master's father-in-law, Mr. William Hamilton.

The plan we finally concluded upon was, to get a large canoe belonging to Mr. Hamilton, and upon the Saturday night previous to Easter holidays, paddle directly up the Chesapeake Bay. On our arrival at the head of the bay, a distance of seventy or eighty miles from where we lived, it was our purpose to turn our canoe adrift, and follow the guidance of the north star till we got beyond the limits of Maryland. Our reason for taking the water route was, that we were less liable to be suspected as runaways; we hoped to be regarded as fishermen; whereas, if we should take the land route, we should be subjected to interruptions of almost every kind. Any one having a white face, and being so disposed, could stop us, and subject us to examination.

The week before our intended start, I wrote several protections, one for each of us. As well as I can remember, they were in the following words, to wit:—

This is to certify that I, the undersigned, have given the bearer, my servant, full liberty to go to Baltimore, and spend the Easter holidays. Written with mine own hand, &c., 1835.

William Hamilton,
Near St. Michael's, in Talbot county, Maryland.

---

*A near-quotation from Shakespeare's *Hamlet* (act 3, scene 1).

We were not going to Baltimore; but, in going up the bay, we went toward Baltimore, and these protections were only intended to protect us while on the bay.

As the time drew near for our departure, our anxiety became more and more intense. It was truly a matter of life and death with us. The strength of our determination was about to be fully tested. At this time, I was very active in explaining every difficulty, removing every doubt, dispelling every fear, and inspiring all with the firmness indispensable to success in our undertaking; assuring them that half was gained the instant we made the move; we had talked long enough; we were now ready to move; if not now, we never should be; and if we did not intend to move now, we had as well fold our arms, sit down, and acknowledge ourselves fit only to be slaves. This, none of us were prepared to acknowledge. Every man stood firm; and at our last meeting, we pledged ourselves afresh, in the most solemn manner, that, at the time appointed, we would certainly start in pursuit of freedom. This was in the middle of the week, at the end of which we were to be off. We went, as usual, to our several fields of labor, but with bosoms highly agitated with thoughts of our truly hazardous undertaking. We tried to conceal our feelings as much as possible; and I think we succeeded very well.

After a painful waiting, the Saturday morning, whose night was to witness our departure, came. I hailed it with joy, bring what of sadness it might. Friday night was a sleepless one for me. I probably felt more anxious than the rest, because I was, by common consent, at the head of the whole affair. The responsibility of success or failure lay heavily upon me. The glory of the one, and the confusion of the other, were alike mine. The first two hours of that morning were such as I never experienced before, and hope never to again. Early in the morning, we went, as usual, to the field. We were spreading manure; and all at once, while thus engaged, I was overwhelmed with an indescribable feeling, in the fulness of which I turned to Sandy, who was near by, and said, "We are betrayed!" "Well," said he, "that thought has this moment struck me." We said no more. I was never more certain of any thing.[34]

The horn was blown as usual, and we went up from the field to the house for breakfast. I went for the form, more than for want of any thing to eat that morning. Just as I got to the house, in looking out at the lane gate, I saw four white men, with two colored men. The white men were on horseback, and the colored ones were walking behind, as if tied. I watched them a few moments till they got up to our lane gate. Here they halted, and tied the colored men to the gate-post. I was not yet certain as to what the matter was. In a few moments, in rode Mr. Hamilton, with a speed betokening great excitement. He came to the door, and inquired if Master William was in. He was told he was at the barn. Mr. Hamilton, without dismounting, rode up to the barn with extraordinary speed. In a few moments, he and Mr. Freeland returned to the house. By this time, the three constables rode up, and in great haste dismounted, tied their horses, and met Master William and Mr. Hamilton returning from the barn; and after talking awhile, they all walked up to the kitchen door. There was no one in the kitchen but myself and John. Henry and Sandy were up at the barn. Mr. Freeland put his head in at the door, and called me by name, saying, there were some gentlemen at the door who wished to see me. I stepped to the door, and inquired what they wanted. They at once seized me, and, without giving me any satisfaction, tied me—lashing my hands closely together. I insisted upon knowing what the matter was. They at length said, that they had learned I had been in a "scrape," and that I was to be examined before my master; and if their information proved false, I should not be hurt.

In a few moments, they succeeded in tying John. They then turned to Henry, who had by this time returned, and commanded him to cross his hands. "I won't!" said Henry, in a firm tone, indicating his readiness to meet the consequences of his refusal. "Won't you?" said Tom Graham, the constable. "No, I won't!" said Henry, in a still stronger tone. With this, two of the constables pulled out their shining pistols, and swore, by their Creator, that they would make him cross his hands or kill him. Each cocked his pistol, and, with fingers on the trigger, walked up to Henry, saying, at the same time, if he did not cross his hands, they would blow his damned heart out. "Shoot me, shoot me!" said Henry; "you can't kill me but once. Shoot, shoot,—and be damned! *I won't be tied!*" This he said in a tone of loud defiance; and at the same time, with a motion as quick as lightning, he with one single stroke dashed the pistols from the hand of each constable. As he did this, all hands fell upon him, and, after beating him some time, they finally overpowered him, and got him tied.

During the scuffle, I managed, I know not how, to get my pass out, and, without being discovered, put it into the fire. We were all now tied; and just as we were to leave for Easton jail, Betsy Freeland, mother of William Freeland, came to the door with her hands full of biscuits, and divided them between Henry and John. She then delivered herself of a speech, to the following effect:—addressing herself to me, she said, "*You devil! You yellow devil!* it was you that put it into the heads of Henry and John to run away. But for you, you long-legged mulatto devil!³⁵ Henry nor John would never have thought of such a thing." I made no reply, and was immediately hurried off towards St. Michael's. Just a moment previous to the scuffle with Henry, Mr. Hamilton suggested the propriety of making a search for the protections which he had understood Frederick had written for himself and the rest. But, just at the moment he was about carrying his proposal into effect, his aid was needed in helping to tie Henry; and the excitement attending the scuffle caused them either to forget, or to deem it unsafe, under the circumstances, to search. So we were not yet convicted of the intention to run away.

When we got about half way to St. Michael's, while the constables having us in charge were looking ahead, Henry inquired of me what he should do with his pass. I told him to eat it with his biscuit, and own nothing; and we passed the word around, "*Own nothing;*" and "*Own nothing!*"³⁶ said we all. Our confidence in each other was unshaken. We were resolved to succeed or fail together, after the calamity had befallen us as much as before. We were now prepared for any thing. We were to be dragged that morning fifteen miles behind horses, and then to be placed in the Easton jail. When we reached St. Michael's, we underwent a sort of examination. We all denied that we ever intended to run away. We did this more to bring out the evidence against us, than from any hope of getting clear of being sold; for, as I have said, we were ready for that. The fact was, we cared but little where we went, so we went together. Our greatest concern was about separation. We dreaded that more than any thing this side of death. We found the evidence against us to be the testimony of one person; our master would not tell who it was; but we came to a unanimous decision among ourselves as to who their informant was. We were sent off to the jail at Easton. When we got there, we were delivered up to the sheriff, Mr. Joseph Graham, and by him placed in jail. Henry, John, and myself, were placed in one room together—Charles, and Henry Bailey, in another. Their object in separating us was to hinder concert.

We had been in jail scarcely twenty minutes, when a swarm of slave traders, and agents for slave traders, flocked into jail to look at us, and to ascertain if we were for sale. Such a set of beings I never saw before! I felt myself surrounded by so many fiends from perdition. A band of pirates never looked more like their father, the devil. They laughed and grinned over us, saying, "Ah, my boys! we have got you, haven't we?" And after taunting us in various ways, they one by one went into an examination of us, with intent to ascertain our value. They would impudently ask us if we would not like to have them for our masters. We would make them no answer, and leave them to find out as best they could. Then they would curse and swear at us, telling us that they could take the devil out of us in a very little while, if we were only in their hands.

While in jail, we found ourselves in much more comfortable quarters than we expected when we went there. We did not get much to eat, nor that which was very good; but we had a good clean room, from the windows of which we could see what was going on in the street, which was very much better than though we had been placed in one of the dark, damp cells. Upon the whole, we got along very well, so far as the jail and its keeper were concerned. Immediately after the holidays were over, contrary to all our expectations, Mr. Hamilton and Mr. Freeland came up to Easton, and took Charles, the two Henrys, and John, out of jail, and carried them home, leaving me alone. I regarded this separation as a final one. It caused me more pain than any thing else in the whole transaction. I was ready for any thing rather than separation. I supposed that they had consulted together, and had decided that, as I was the whole cause of the intention of the others to run away, it was hard to make the innocent suffer with the guilty; and that they had, therefore, concluded to take the others home, and sell me, as a warning to the others that remained. It is due to the noble Henry to say, he seemed almost as reluctant at leaving the prison as at leaving home to come to the prison. But we knew we should, in all probability, be separated, if we were sold; and since he was in their hands, he concluded to go peaceably home.

I was now left to my fate. I was all alone, and within the walls of a stone prison. But a few days before, and I was full of hope. I expected to have been safe in a land of freedom; but now I was covered with gloom, sunk down to the utmost despair. I thought the possibility of freedom was gone. I was kept in this way about one week, at the end of which, Captain Auld, my master, to my surprise and utter astonishment, came up, and took me out, with the intention of sending me, with a gentleman of his acquaintance, into Alabama. But, from some cause or other, he did not send me to Alabama, but concluded to send me back to Baltimore, to live again with his brother Hugh, and to learn a trade.

Thus, after an absence of three years and one month, I was once more permitted to return to my old home at Baltimore. My master sent me away, because there existed against me a very great prejudice in the community, and he feared I might be killed.

In a few weeks after I went to Baltimore, Master Hugh hired me to Mr. William Gardner, an extensive ship-builder, on Fell's Point. I was put there to learn how to calk. It, however, proved a very unfavorable place for the accomplishment of this object. Mr. Gardner was engaged that spring in building two large man-of-war brigs, professedly for the Mexican government. The vessels were to be launched in the July of that year, and in failure thereof, Mr. Gardner was to lose a considerable sum; so that when I entered, all was hurry. There was no time to learn any thing. Every man had to do that which he knew how to do. In entering the ship-yard, my orders from Mr. Gardner were, to do whatever the carpenters commanded me to do. This was placing me at the beck and call of about seventy-five men. I was to regard all these as masters. Their word was to be my law. My situation was a most trying one. At times I needed a dozen pair of hands. I was called a dozen ways in the space of a single minute. Three or four voices would strike my ear at the same moment. It was—"Fred., come help me to cant this timber* here."—"Fred., come carry this timber yonder."—"Fred., bring that roller here."—"Fred., go get a fresh can of water."—"Fred., come help saw off the end of this timber."—

---

*Toss or turn over a piece of timber.

"Fred., go quick, and get the crowbar."—"Fred., hold on the end of this fall."—"Fred., go to the blacksmith's shop, and get a new punch."—"Hurra, Fred.! run and bring me a cold chisel."—"I say, Fred., bear a hand, and get up a fire as quick as lightning under that steam-box."—"Halloo, nigger! come, turn this grindstone."— "Come, come! move, move! and *bowse** this timber forward."—"I say, darky, blast your eyes, why don't you heat up some pitch?"—"Halloo! halloo! halloo!" (Three voices at the same time.) "Come here!—Go there!—Hold on where you are! Damn you, if you move, I'll knock your brains out!"

This was my school for eight months; and I might have remained there longer, but for a most horrid fight I had with four of the white apprentices, in which my left eye was nearly knocked out, and I was horribly mangled in other respects. The facts in the case were these: Until a very little while after I went there, white and black ship-carpenters worked side by side, and no one seemed to see any impropriety in it. All hands seemed to be very well satisfied. Many of the black carpenters were free men. Things seemed to be going on very well. All at once, the white carpenters knocked off, and said they would not work with free colored workmen. Their reason for this, as alleged, was, that if free colored carpenters were encouraged, they would soon take the trade into their own hands, and poor white men would be thrown out of employment. They therefore felt called upon at once to put a stop to it. And, taking advantage of Mr. Gardner's necessities, they broke off, swearing they would work no longer, unless he would discharge his black carpenters. Now, though this did not extend to me in form, it did reach me in fact. My fellow-apprentices very soon began to feel it degrading to them to work with me. They began to put on airs, and talk about the "niggers" taking the country, saying we all ought to be killed; and, being encouraged by the journeymen, they commenced making my condition as hard as they could, by hectoring me around, and sometimes striking me. I, of course, kept the vow I made after the fight with Mr. Covey, and struck back again, regardless of consequences; and while I kept them from combining, I succeeded very well; for I could whip the whole of

---

*Pull, haul.

them, taking them separately. They, howevet, at length combined, and came upon me, armed with sticks, stones, and heavy handspikes. One came in front with a half brick. There was one at each side of me, and one behind me. While I was attending to those in front, and on either side, the one behind ran up with the handspike, and struck me a heavy blow upon the head. It stunned me. I fell, and with this they all ran upon me, and fell to beating me with their fists. I let them lay on for a while, gathering strength. In an instant, I gave a sudden surge, and rose to my hands and knees. Just as I did that, one of their number gave me, with his heavy boot, a powerful kick in the left eye. My eyeball seemed to have burst. When they saw my eye closed, and badly swollen, they left me. With this I seized the handspike, and for a time pursued them. But here the carpenters interfered, and I thought I might as well give it up. It was impossible to stand my hand against so many. All this took place in sight of not less than fifty white ship-carpenters, and not one interposed a friendly word; but some cried, "Kill the damned nigger! Kill him! kill him! He struck a white person." I found my only chance for life was in flight. I succeeded in getting away without an additional blow, and barely so; for to strike a white man is death by Lynch law,[37]—and that was the law in Mr. Gardner's ship-yard; nor is there much of any other out of Mr. Gardner's ship-yard.

I went directly home, and told the story of my wrongs to Master Hugh; and I am happy to say of him, irreligious as he was, his conduct was heavenly, compared with that of his brother Thomas under similar circumstances. He listened attentively to my narration of the circumstances leading to the savage outrage, and gave many proofs of his strong indignation at it. The heart of my once overkind mistress was again melted into pity. My puffed-out eye and blood-covered face moved her to tears. She took a chair by me, washed the blood from my face, and, with a mother's tenderness, bound up my head, covering the wounded eye with a lean piece of fresh beef. It was almost compensation for my suffering to witness, once more, a manifestation of kindness from this, my once affectionate old mistress. Master Hugh was very much enraged. He gave expression to his feelings by pouring out curses upon the heads of those who did the deed. As soon as I got a little the better of my bruises, he took me with him to Esquire Watson's, on Bond Street, to see what could be done about

the matter. Mr. Watson inquired who saw the assault committed.
Master Hugh told him it was done in Mr. Gardner's ship-yard, at
midday, where there were a large company of men at work. "As to
that," he said, "the deed was done, and there was no question as to
who did it." His answer was, he could do nothing in the case, unless
some white man would come forward and testify. He could issue no
warrant on my word. If I had been killed in the presence of a thousand colored people, their testimony combined would have been in-
sufficient to have arrested one of the murderers. Master Hugh, for
once, was compelled to say this state of things was too bad. Of
course, it was impossible to get any white man to volunteer his testimony in my behalf, and against the white young men. Even those
who may have sympathized with me were not prepared to do this. It
required a degree of courage unknown to them to do so; for just at
that time, the slightest manifestation of humanity toward a colored
person was denounced as abolitionism, and that name subjected its
bearer to frightful liabilities. The watchwords of the bloody-minded
in that region, and in those days, were, "Damn the abolitionists!" and
"Damn the niggers!" There was nothing done, and probably nothing
would have been done if I had been killed. Such was, and such remains, the state of things in the Christian city of Baltimore.

Master Hugh, finding he could get no redress, refused to let me
go back again to Mr. Gardner. He kept me himself, and his wife
dressed my wound till I was again restored to health. He then took
me into the ship-yard of which he was foreman, in the employment
of Mr. Walter Price. There I was immediately set to calking, and very
soon learned the art of using my mallet and irons.* In the course of
one year from the time I left Mr. Gardner's, I was able to command
the highest wages given to the most experienced calkers. I was now
of some importance to my master. I was bringing him from six to
seven dollars per week. I sometimes brought him nine dollars per
week: my wages were a dollar and a half a day. After learning how to
calk, I sought my own employment, made my own contracts, and
collected the money which I earned. My pathway became much
more smooth than before; my condition was now much more com-

*Tools of the blacksmith.

fortable. When I could get no calking to do, I did nothing. During these leisure times, those old notions about freedom would steal over me again. When in Mr. Gardner's employment, I was kept in such a perpetual whirl of excitement, I could think of nothing, scarcely, but my life; and in thinking of my life, I almost forgot my liberty. I have observed this in my experience of slavery,—that whenever my condition was improved, instead of its increasing my contentment, it only increased my desire to be free, and set me to thinking of plans to gain my freedom. I have found that, to make a contented slave, it is necessary to make a thoughtless one. It is necessary to darken his moral and mental vision, and, as far as possible, to annihilate the power of reason. He must be able to detect no inconsistencies in slavery; he must be made to feel that slavery is right; and he can be brought to that only when he ceases to be a man.

I was now getting, as I have said, one dollar and fifty cents per day. I contracted for it; I earned it; it was paid to me; it was rightfully my own; yet, upon each returning Saturday night, I was compelled to deliver every cent of that money to Master Hugh. And why? Not because he earned it,—not because he had any hand in earning it,—not because I owed it to him,—nor because he possessed the slightest shadow of a right to it; but solely because he had the power to compel me to give it up. The right of the grim-visaged pirate upon the high seas is exactly the same.

CHAPTER XI

I NOW COME TO that part of my life during which I planned, and finally succeeded in making, my escape from slavery. But before narrating any of the peculiar circumstances, I deem it proper to make known my intention not to state all the facts connected with the transaction. My reasons for pursuing this course may be understood from the following: First, were I to give a minute statement of all the facts, it is not only possible, but quite probable, that others would thereby be involved in the most embarrassing difficulties. Secondly, such a statement would most undoubtedly induce greater vigilance on the part of slaveholders than has existed heretofore among them; which would, of course, be the means of guarding a door whereby some dear brother bondman might escape his galling chains. I deeply regret the necessity that impels me to suppress any thing of importance connected with my experience in slavery. It would afford me great pleasure indeed, as well as materially add to the interest of my narrative, were I at liberty to gratify a curiosity, which I know exists in the minds of many, by an accurate statement of all the facts pertaining to my most fortunate escape. But I must deprive myself of this pleasure, and the curious of the gratification which such a statement would afford. I would allow myself to suffer under the greatest imputations which evil-minded men might suggest, rather than exculpate myself,* and thereby run the hazard of closing the slightest avenue by which a brother slave might clear himself of the chains and fetters of slavery.

I have never approved of the very public manner in which some of our western friends have conducted what they call the *underground railroad*,[38] but which, I think, by their open declarations, has been made most emphatically the *upperground railroad*. I honor those good men and women for their noble daring, and applaud them for willingly subjecting themselves to bloody persecution, by openly avowing their participation in the escape of slaves. I, however, can see very lit-

---

*Prove myself blameless.

tle good resulting from such a course, either to themselves or the slaves escaping; while, upon the other hand, I see and feel assured that those open declarations are a positive evil to the slaves remaining, who are seeking to escape. They do nothing towards enlightening the slave, whilst they do much towards enlightening the master. They stimulate him to greater watchfulness, and enhance his power to capture his slave. We owe something to the slaves south of the line as well as to those north of it; and in aiding the latter on their way to freedom, we should be careful to do nothing which would be likely to hinder the former from escaping from slavery. I would keep the merciless slaveholder profoundly ignorant of the means of flight adopted by the slave. I would leave him to imagine himself surrounded by myriads of invisible tormentors, ever ready to snatch from his infernal grasp his trembling prey. Let him be left to feel his way in the dark; let darkness commensurate with his crime hover over him; and let him feel that at every step he takes, in pursuit of the flying bondman, he is running the frightful risk of having his hot brains dashed out by an invisible agency. Let us render the tyrant no aid; let us not hold the light by which he can trace the footprints of our flying brother. But enough of this. I will now proceed to the statement of those facts, connected with my escape, for which I am alone responsible, and for which no one can be made to suffer but myself.

In the early part of the year 1838, I became quite restless. I could see no reason why I should, at the end of each week, pour the reward of my toil into the purse of my master. When I carried to him my weekly wages, he would, after counting the money, look me in the face with a robber-like fierceness, and ask, "Is this all?" He was satisfied with nothing less than the last cent. He would, however, when I made him six dollars, sometimes give me six cents, to encourage me. It had the opposite effect. I regarded it as a sort of admission of my right to the whole. The fact that he gave me any part of my wages was proof, to my mind, that he believed me entitled to the whole of them. I always felt worse for having received any thing; for I feared that the giving me a few cents would ease his conscience, and make him feel himself to be a pretty honorable sort of robber. My discontent grew upon me. I was ever on the look-out for means of escape; and, finding no direct means, I determined to try to hire my time, with a view of getting money with which to make my escape. In the spring of 1838, when Master Thomas came to Baltimore to purchase his spring goods, I got an opportunity, and applied to him to allow me to hire my time. He unhesitatingly refused my request, and told me this was another stratagem by which to escape. He told me I could go nowhere but that he could get me; and that, in the event of my running away, he should spare no pains in his efforts to catch me. He exhorted me to content myself, and be obedient. He told me, if I would be happy, I must lay out no plans for the future. He said, if I behaved myself properly, he would take care of me. Indeed, he advised me to complete thoughtlessness of the future, and taught me to depend solely upon him for happiness. He seemed to see fully the pressing necessity of setting aside my intellectual nature, in order to contentment in slavery. But in spite of him, and even in spite of myself, I continued to think, and to think about the injustice of my enslavement, and the means of escape.

About two months after this, I applied to Master Hugh for the privilege of hiring my time. He was not acquainted with the fact that I had applied to Master Thomas, and had been refused. He too, at first, seemed disposed to refuse; but, after some reflection, he granted me the privilege, and proposed the following terms: I was to be allowed all my time, make all contracts with those for whom I worked, and find my own employment; and, in return for this liberty, I was to pay him three dollars at the end of each week; find myself in calking tools, and in board and clothing. My board was two dollars and a half per week. This, with the wear and tear of clothing and calking tools, made my regular expenses about six dollars per week. This amount I was compelled to make up, or relinquish the privilege of hiring my time. Rain or shine, work or no work, at the end of each week the money must be forthcoming, or I must give up my privilege. This arrangement, it will be perceived, was decidedly in my master's favor. It relieved him of all need of looking after me. His money was sure. He received all the benefits of slaveholding without its evils; while I endured all the evils of a slave, and suffered all the care and anxiety of a freeman. I found it a hard bargain. But, hard as it was, I thought it better than the old mode of getting along. It was a step towards freedom to be allowed to bear the responsibilities of a freeman, and I was determined to hold on upon it. I bent myself to the work of making money. I was ready to work at night as well as day, and by the most untiring perseverance and industry, I made enough to meet my expenses, and lay up a little money every week. I went on thus from May till August. Master Hugh then refused to allow me to hire my time longer. The ground for his refusal was a failure on my part, one Saturday night, to pay him for my week's time. This failure was occasioned by my attending a camp meeting about ten miles from Baltimore. During the week, I had entered into an engagement with a number of young friends to start from Baltimore to the camp ground early Saturday evening; and being detained by my employer, I was unable to get down to Master Hugh's without disappointing the company. I knew that Master Hugh was in no special need of the money that night. I therefore decided to go to camp meeting, and upon my return pay him the three dollars. I staid [sic] at the camp meeting one day longer than I intended when I left. But as soon as I returned, I called upon him to pay him what he considered his due. I found him very angry; he could scarce restrain his wrath. He said he had a great mind to give me a severe whipping. He wished to know how I dared go out of the city without asking his permission. I told him I hired my time, and while I paid him the price which he asked for it, I did not know that I was bound to ask him when and where I should go. This reply troubled him; and, after reflecting a few moments, he turned to me, and said I should hire my time no longer; that the next thing he should know of, I would be running away. Upon the same plea, he told me to bring my tools and clothing home forthwith. I did so; but instead of seeking work, as I had been accustomed to do previously to hiring my time, I spent the whole week without the performance of a single stroke of work. I did this in retaliation. Saturday night, he called upon me as usual for my week's wages. I told him I had no wages; I had done no work that week. Here we were upon the point of coming to blows. He raved, and swore his determination to get hold of me. I did not allow myself a single word; but was resolved, if he laid the weight of his hand upon me, it should be blow for blow. He did not strike me, but told me that he would find me in constant employment in future. I thought the matter over during the next day, Sunday, and finally resolved upon the third day of September, as the day upon which I would make a second attempt to secure my freedom. I now had three weeks during which to prepare for my journey. Early on Monday morning, before

Master Hugh had time to make any engagement for me, I went out and got employment of Mr. Butler, at his ship-yard near the draw-bridge, upon what is called the City Block, thus making it unneces-sary for him to seek employment for me. At the end of the week, I brought him between eight and nine dollars. He seemed very well pleased, and asked me why I did not do the same the week before. He little knew what my plans were. My object in working steadily was to remove any suspicion he might entertain of my intent to run away; and in this I succeeded admirably. I suppose he thought I was never better satisfied with my condition than at the very time during which I was planning my escape. The second week passed, and again I carried him my full wages; and so well pleased was he, that he gave me twenty-five cents, (quite a large sum for a slaveholder to give a slave,) and bade me to make a good use of it. I told him I would.

Things went on without very smoothly indeed, but within there was trouble. It is impossible for me to describe my feelings as the time of my contemplated start drew near. I had a number of warm-hearted friends in Baltimore,—friends that I loved almost as I did my life,—and the thought of being separated from them forever was painful beyond expression. It is my opinion that thousands would es-cape from slavery, who now remain, but for the strong cords of af-fection that bind them to their friends. The thought of leaving my friends was decidedly the most painful thought with which I had to contend. The love of them was my tender point, and shook my deci-sion more than all things else. Besides the pain of separation, the dread and apprehension of a failure exceeded what I had experienced at my first attempt. The appalling defeat I then sustained returned to torment me. I felt assured that, if I failed in this attempt, my case would be a hopeless one—it would seal my fate as a slave forever. I could not hope to get off with any thing less than the severest pun-ishment, and being placed beyond the means of escape. It required no very vivid imagination to depict the most frightful scenes through which I should have to pass, in case I failed. The wretchedness of slavery, and the blessedness of freedom, were perpetually before me. It was life and death with me. But I remained firm, and, according to my resolution, on the third day of September, 1838, I left my chains, and succeeded in reaching New York without the slightest interrup-tion of any kind. How I did so,—what means I adopted,—what direction I travelled, and by what mode of conveyance,—I must leave unexplained, for the reasons before mentioned.

I have been frequently asked how I felt when I found myself in a free State. I have never been able to answer the question with any satisfaction to myself. It was a moment of the highest excitement I ever experienced. I suppose I felt as one may imagine the unarmed mariner to feel when he is rescued by a friendly man-of-war from the pursuit of a pirate. In writing to a dear friend, immediately after my arrival at New York, I said I felt like one who had escaped a den of hungry lions. This state of mind, however, very soon subsided; and I was again seized with a feeling of great insecurity and loneliness. I was yet liable to be taken back, and subjected to all the tortures of slavery. This in itself was enough to damp the ardor of my enthusiasm. But the loneliness overcame me. There I was in the midst of thousands, and yet a perfect stranger; without home and without friends, in the midst of thousands of my own brethren—children of a common Father, and yet I dared not to unfold to any one of them my sad condition. I was afraid to speak to any one for fear of speaking to the wrong one, and thereby falling into the hands of money-loving kidnappers, whose business it was to lie in wait for the panting fugitive, as the ferocious beasts of the forest lie in wait for their prey. The motto which I adopted when I started from slavery was this—"Trust no man!" I saw in every white man an enemy, and in almost every colored man cause for distrust. It was a most painful situation; and, to understand it, one must needs experience it, or imagine himself in similar circumstances. Let him be a fugitive slave in a strange land—a land given up to be the hunting-ground for slaveholders—whose inhabitants are legalized kidnappers—where he is every moment subjected to the terrible liability of being seized upon by his fellow-men, as the hideous crocodile seizes upon his prey!—I say, let him place himself in my situation—without home or friends—without money or credit—wanting shelter, and no one to give it—wanting bread, and no money to buy it,—and at the same time let him feel that he is pursued by merciless men-hunters, and in total darkness as to what to do, where to go, or where to stay,—perfectly helpless both as to the means of defence and means of escape,—in the midst of plenty, yet suffering the terrible gnawings of hunger,—in the midst of houses, yet having no home,—among fellow-men, yet feeling as if in the midst of wild beasts, whose greediness to swallow up the trembling and half-famished fugitive is only equalled by that with which the monsters of the deep swallow up the helpless fish upon which they subsist,—I say, let him be placed in this most trying situation,—the situation in which I was placed,—then, and not till then, will he fully appreciate the hardships of, and know how to sympathize with, the toil-worn and whip-scarred fugitive slave.

Thank Heaven, I remained but a short time in this distressed situation. I was relieved from it by the humane hand of MR. DAVID RUGGLES,[39] whose vigilance, kindness, and perseverance, I shall never forget. I am glad of an opportunity to express, as far as words can, the love and gratitude I bear him. Mr. Ruggles is now afflicted with blindness, and is himself in need of the same kind offices which he was once so forward in the performance of toward others. I had been in New York but a few days, when Mr. Ruggles sought me out, and very kindly took me to his boarding-house at the corner of Church and Lespenard Streets. Mr. Ruggles was then very deeply engaged in the memorable *Darg* case,[40] as well as attending to a number of other fugitive slaves, devising ways and means for their successful escape; and, though watched and hemmed in on almost every side, he seemed to be more than a match for his enemies.

Very soon after I went to Mr. Ruggles, he wished to know of me where I wanted to go; as he deemed it unsafe for me to remain in New York. I told him I was a calker, and should like to go where I could get work. I thought of going to Canada; but he decided against it, and in favor of my going to New Bedford, thinking I should be able to get work there at my trade. At this time, Anna, my intended wife,[41] came on; for I wrote to her immediately after my arrival at New York, (notwithstanding my homeless, houseless, and helpless condition,) informing her of my successful flight, and wishing her to come on forthwith. In a few days after her arrival, Mr. Ruggles called in the Rev. J. W. C. Pennington, who, in the presence of Mr. Ruggles, Mrs. Michaels, and two or three others, performed the marriage ceremony, and gave us a certificate, of which the following is an exact copy:—

THIS may certify, that I joined together in holy matrimony Frederick Johnson* and Anna Murray, as man and wife, in the presence of Mr. David Ruggles and Mrs. Michaels.

James W. C. Pennington.[42]
New York, Sept. 15, 1838.

Upon receiving this certificate, and a five-dollar bill from Mr. Ruggles, I shouldered one part of our baggage, and Anna took up the other, and we set out forthwith to take passage on board of the steamboat John W Richmond for Newport, on our way to New Bedford. Mr. Ruggles gave me a letter to a Mr. Shaw in Newport, and told me, in case my money did not serve me to New Bedford, to stop in Newport and obtain further assistance; but upon our arrival at Newport, we were so anxious to get to a place of safety, that, notwithstanding we lacked the necessary money to pay our fare, we decided to take seats in the stage, and promise to pay when we got to New Bedford. We were encouraged to do this by two excellent gentlemen, residents of New Bedford, whose names I afterward ascertained to be Joseph Ricketson and William C. Taber. They seemed at once to understand our circumstances, and gave us such assurance of their friendliness as put us fully at ease in their presence. It was good indeed to meet with such friends, at such a time. Upon reaching New Bedford, we were directed to the house of Mr. Nathan Johnson, by whom we were kindly received, and hospitably provided for. Both Mr. and Mrs. Johnson took a deep and lively interest in our welfare. They proved themselves quite worthy of the name of abolitionists. When the stage-driver found us unable to pay our fare, he held on upon our baggage as security for the debt. I had but to mention the fact to Mr. Johnson, and he forthwith advanced the money.

We now began to feel a degree of safety, and to prepare ourselves for the duties and responsibilities of a life of freedom. On the morning after our arrival at New Bedford, while at the breakfast-table, the question arose as to what name I should be called by. The name given me by my mother was, "Frederick Augustus Washington Bailey." I, however, had dispensed with the two middle names long before I left Maryland so that I was generally known by the name of "Frederick

*Author's note: I had changed my name from Frederick *Bailey* to that of *Johnson*.

Bailey." I started from Baltimore bearing the name of "Stanley." When
I got to New York, I again changed my name to "Frederick Johnson,"
and thought that would be the last change. But when I got to New
Bedford, I found it necessary again to change my name. The reason of
this necessity was, that there were so many Johnsons in New Bedford,
it was already quite difficult to distinguish between them. I gave Mr.
Johnson the privilege of choosing me a name, but told him he must
not take from me the name of "Frederick." I must hold on to that, to
preserve a sense of my identity. Mr. Johnson had just been reading the
"Lady of the Lake," and at once suggested that my name be "Douglass."[43] From that time until now I have been called "Frederick Douglass;" and as I am more widely known by that name than by either of
the others, I shall continue to use it as my own.

I was quite disappointed at the general appearance of things in New
Bedford.[44] The impression which I had received respecting the character and condition of the people of the north, I found to be singularly er-
roneous. I had very strangely supposed, while in slavery, that few of
the comforts, and scarcely any of the luxuries, of life were enjoyed at the
north, compared with what were enjoyed by the slaveholders of the
south. I probably came to this conclusion from the fact that northern
people owned no slaves. I supposed that they were about upon a level
with the non-slaveholding population of the south. I knew *they* were exceedingly poor, and I had been accustomed to regard their poverty as
the necessary consequence of their being non-slaveholders. I had somehow imbibed the opinion that, in the absence of slaves, there could be
no wealth, and very little refinement. And upon coming to the north, I
expected to meet with a rough, hard-handed, and uncultivated population, living in the most Spartan-like simplicity, knowing nothing of the
ease, luxury, pomp, and grandeur of southern slaveholders. Such being
my conjectures, any one acquainted with the appearance of New Bedford may very readily infer how palpably I must have seen my mistake.

In the afternoon of the day when I reached New Bedford, I visited
the wharves, to take a view of the shipping. Here I found myself surrounded with the strongest proofs of wealth. Lying at the wharves,
and riding in the stream, I saw many ships of the finest model, in the
best order, and of the largest size. Upon the right and left, I was walled
in by granite warehouses of the widest dimensions, stowed to their utmost capacity with the necessaries and comforts of life. Added to this,

almost every body seemed to be at work, but noiselessly so, compared with what I had been accustomed to in Baltimore. There were no loud songs heard from those engaged in loading and unloading ships. I heard no deep oaths or horrid curses on the laborer. I saw no whipping of men; but all seemed to go smoothly on. Every man appeared to understand his work, and went at it with a sober, yet cheerful earnestness, which betokened the deep interest which he felt in what he was doing, as well as a sense of his own dignity as a man. To me this looked exceedingly strange. From the wharves I strolled around and over the town, gazing with wonder and admiration at the splendid churches, beautiful dwellings, and finely-cultivated gardens; evincing an amount of wealth, comfort, taste, and refinement, such as I had never seen in any part of slaveholding Maryland.

Every thing looked clean, new, and beautiful. I saw few or no dilapidated houses, with poverty-stricken inmates; no half-naked children and barefooted women, such as I had been accustomed to see in Hillsborough, Easton, St. Michael's, and Baltimore. The people looked more able, stronger, healthier, and happier, than those of Maryland. I was for once made glad by a view of extreme wealth, without being saddened by seeing extreme poverty. But the most astonishing as well as the most interesting thing to me was the condition of the colored people, a great many of whom, like myself, had escaped thither as a refuge from the hunters of men. I found many, who had not been seven years out of their chains, living in finer houses, and evidently enjoying more of the comforts of life, than the average of slaveholders in Maryland. I will venture to assert that my friend Mr. Nathan Johnson (of whom I can say with a grateful heart, "I was hungry, and he gave me meat; I was thirsty, and he gave me drink; I was a stranger, and he took me in")* lived in a neater house; dined at a better table; took, paid for, and read, more newspapers; better understood the moral, religious, and political character of the nation,—than nine tenths of the slaveholders in Talbot county, Maryland. Yet Mr. Johnson was a working man. His hands were hardened by toil, and not his alone, but those also of Mrs. Johnson. I found the colored people much more spirited than I had supposed they would be. I found among them a determination to protect each other from the blood-thirsty kidnapper, at all hazards. Soon

---

*Reference to the Bible, Matthew 25:35.

after my arrival, I was told of a circumstance which illustrated their spirit. A colored man and a fugitive slave were on unfriendly terms. The former was heard to threaten the latter with informing his master of his whereabouts. Straightway a meeting was called among the colored people, under the stereotyped notice, "Business of importance!" The betrayer was invited to attend. The people came at the appointed hour, and organized the meeting by appointing a very religious old gentleman as president, who, I believe, made a prayer, after which he addressed the meeting as follows: *"Friends, we have got him here, and I would recommend that you young men just take him outside the door, and kill him!"* With this, a number of them bolted at him; but they were intercepted by some more timid than themselves, and the betrayer escaped their vengeance, and has not been seen in New Bedford since. I believe there have been no more such threats, and should there be hereafter, I doubt not that death would be the consequence.

I found employment, the third day after my arrival, in stowing a sloop with a load of oil. It was new, dirty, and hard work for me; but I went at it with a glad heart and a willing hand. I was now my own master. It was a happy moment, the rapture of which can be understood only by those who have been slaves. It was the first work, the reward of which was to be entirely my own. There was no Master Hugh standing ready, the moment I earned the money, to rob me of it. I worked that day with a pleasure I had never before experienced. I was at work for myself and newly-married wife. It was to me the starting-point of a new existence. When I got through with that job, I went in pursuit of a job of calking; but such was the strength of prejudice against color, among the white calkers, that they refused to work with me, and of course I could get no employment.* Finding my trade of no immediate benefit, I threw off my calking habiliments,† and prepared myself to do any kind of work I could get to do. Mr. Johnson kindly let me have his woodhorse and saw, and I very soon found myself a plenty of work. There was no work too hard—none too dirty. I was ready to saw wood, shovel coal, carry the hod,‡ sweep the chim-

---

*Author's note: I am told that colored persons can now get employment at calking in New Bedford—a result of anti-slavery effort.

†Clothes.

‡Receptacle for carrying coal, bricks, or the like.

ney, or roll oil casks,—all of which I did for nearly three years in New Bedford, before I became known to the anti-slavery world.

In about four months after I went to New Bedford, there came a young man to me, and inquired if I did not wish to take the "Liberator."* I told him I did; but, just having made my escape from slavery, I remarked that I was unable to pay for it then. I, however, finally became a subscriber to it. The paper came, and I read it from week to week with such feelings as it would be quite idle for me to attempt to describe. The paper became my meat and my drink. My soul was set all on fire. Its sympathy for my brethren in bonds—its scathing denunciations of slaveholders—its faithful exposures of slavery—and its powerful attacks upon the upholders of the institution—sent a thrill of joy through my soul, such as I had never felt before!

I had not long been a reader of the "Liberator," before I got a pretty correct idea of the principles, measures, and spirit of the anti-slavery reform. I took right hold of the cause. I could do but little; but what I could, I did with a joyful heart, and never felt happier than when in an anti-slavery meeting. I seldom had much to say at the meetings, because what I wanted to say was said so much better by others. But, while attending an anti-slavery convention at Nantucket, on the 11th of August, 1841, I felt strongly moved to speak, and was at the same time much urged to do so by Mr. William C. Coffin, a gentleman who had heard me speak in the colored people's meeting at New Bedford. It was a severe cross, and I took it up reluctantly. The truth was, I felt myself a slave, and the idea of speaking to white people weighed me down. I spoke but a few moments, when I felt a degree of freedom, and said what I desired with considerable ease. From that time until now, I have been engaged in pleading the cause of my brethren—with what success, and with what devotion, I leave those acquainted with my labors to decide.

---

*Widely influential abolitionist newspaper (1831–1865), edited by William Lloyd Garrison.

APPENDIX

I FIND, SINCE READING over the foregoing Narrative that I have, in several instances, spoken in such a tone and manner, respecting religion, as may possibly lead those unacquainted with my religious views to suppose me an opponent of all religion. To remove the liability of such misapprehension, I deem it proper to append the following brief explanation. What I have said respecting and against religion, I mean strictly to apply to the *slaveholding religion* of this land, and with no possible reference to Christianity proper; for, between the Christianity of this land, and the Christianity of Christ, I recognize the widest possible difference—so wide, that to receive the one as good, pure, and holy, is of necessity to reject the other as bad, corrupt, and wicked. To be the friend of the one, is of necessity to be the enemy of the other. I love the pure, peaceable, and impartial Christianity of Christ: I therefore hate the corrupt, slaveholding, women-whipping, cradle-plundering, partial and hypocritical Christianity of this land. Indeed, I can see no reason, but the most deceitful one, for calling the religion of this land Christianity. I look upon it as the climax of all misnomers, the boldest of all frauds, and the grossest of all libels. Never was there a clearer case of "stealing the livery of the court of heaven to serve the devil in."[45] I am filled with unutterable loathing when I contemplate the religious pomp and show, together with the horrible inconsistencies, which every where surround me. We have men-stealers for ministers, women-whippers for missionaries, and cradle-plunderers for church members. The man who wields the blood-clotted cowskin during the week fills the pulpit on Sunday, and claims to be a minister of the meek and lowly Jesus. The man who robs me of my earnings at the end of each week meets me as a class-leader on Sunday morning, to show me the way of life, and the path of salvation. He who sells my sister, for purposes of prostitution, stands forth as the pious advocate of purity. He who proclaims it a religious duty to read the Bible denies me the right of learning to read the name of God who made me. He who is the re-

ligious advocate of marriage robs whole millions of its sacred influence, and leaves them to the ravages of wholesale pollution. The
warm defender of the sacredness of the family relation is the same
that scatters whole families,—sundering husbands and wives, parents
and children, sisters and brothers,—leaving the hut vacant, and the
hearth desolate. We see the thief preaching against theft, and the
adulterer against adultery. We have men sold to build churches,
women sold to support the gospel, and babes sold to purchase Bibles
for the *poor heathen! all for the glory of God and the good of souls!* The
slave auctioneer's bell and the church-going bell chime in with each
other, and the bitter cries of the heart-broken slave are drowned in
the religious shouts of his pious master. Revivals of religion and revivals in the slave-trade go hand in hand together. The slave prison
and the church stand near each other. The clanking of fetters and the
rattling of chains in the prison, and the pious psalm and solemn
prayer in the church, may be heard at the same time. The dealers in
the bodies and souls of men erect their stand in the presence of the
pulpit, and they mutually help each other. The dealer gives his blood-
stained gold to support the pulpit, and the pulpit, in return, covers his
infernal business with the garb of Christianity. Here we have religion
and robbery the allies of each other—devils dressed in angels' robes,
and hell presenting the semblance of paradise.

> Just God! and these are they,
>   Who minister at thine altar, God of right!
> Men who their hands, with prayer and blessing, lay
>   On Israel's ark of light.*
>
> What! preach, and kidnap men?
>   Give thanks, and rob thy own afflicted poor?
> Talk of thy glorious liberty, and then
>   Bolt hard the captive's door?
>
> What! servants of thy own
>   Merciful Son, who came to seek and save

---

*The Holy Ark, which contains the Torah; implicitly, the whole body of law contained
in the Old Testament.

The homeless and the outcast, fettering down
The tasked and plundered slave!

Pilate and Herod friends![46]
Chief priests and rulers, as of old, combine!
Just God and holy! is that church which lends
Strength to the spoiler thine?*

The Christianity of America is a Christianity, of whose votaries† it may be as truly said, as it was of the ancient scribes and Pharisees, "They bind heavy burdens, and grievous to be borne, and lay them on men's shoulders, but they themselves will not move them with one of their fingers. All their works they do for to be seen of men.——They love the uppermost rooms at feasts, and the chief seats in the synagogues, ... and to be called of men, Rabbi, Rabbi.——But woe unto you, scribes and Pharisees, hypocrites! for ye shut up the kingdom of heaven against men; for ye neither go in yourselves, neither suffer ye them that are entering to go in. Ye devour widows' houses, and for a pretence make long prayers; therefore ye shall receive the greater damnation. Ye compass sea and land to make one proselyte, and when he is made, ye make him twofold more the child of hell than yourselves.——Woe unto you, scribes and Pharisees, hypocrites! for ye pay tithe of mint, and anise, and cumin, and have omitted the weightier matters of the law, judgment, mercy, and faith; these ought ye to have done, and not to leave the other undone. Ye blind guides! which strain at a gnat, and swallow a camel. Woe unto you, scribes and Pharisees, hypocrites! for ye make clean the outside of the cup and of the platter; but within, they are full of extortion and excess.—Woe unto you, scribes and Pharisees, hypocrites! for ye are like unto whited sepulchres, which indeed appear beautiful outward, but are within full of dead men's bones, and of all uncleanness. Even so ye also outwardly appear righteous unto men, but within ye are full of hypocrisy and iniquity."‡
Dark and terrible as is this picture, I hold it to be strictly true of the overwhelming mass of professed Christians in America. They

---

*From John Greenleaf Whittier's 1836 poem "Clerical Oppressors."
†Devout worshipers.
‡From the Bible, Matthew 23:4–28 (King James Version).

strain at a gnat, and swallow a camel. Could any thing be more true of our churches? They would be shocked at the proposition of fellowshipping a *sheep*-stealer; and at the same time they hug to their communion a *man*-stealer and brand me with being an infidel, if I find fault with them for it. They attend with Pharisaical strictness to the outward forms of religion, and at the same time neglect the weightier matters of the law, judgment, mercy, and faith. They are always ready to sacrifice, but seldom to show mercy. They are they who are represented as professing to love God whom they have not seen, whilst they hate their brother whom they have seen. They love the heathen on the other side of the globe. They can pray for him, pay money to have the Bible put into his hand, and missionaries to instruct him; while they despise and totally neglect the heathen at their own doors.

Such is, very briefly, my view of the religion of this land; and to avoid any misunderstanding, growing out of the use of general terms, I mean, by the religion of this land, that which is revealed in the words, deeds, and actions, of those bodies, north and south, calling themselves Christian churches, and yet in union with slaveholders. It is against religion, as presented by these bodies, that I have felt it my duty to testify.

I conclude these remarks by copying the following portrait of the religion of the south, (which is, by communion and fellowship, the religion of the north,) which I soberly affirm is "true to the life," and without caricature or the slightest exaggeration. It is said to have been drawn, several years before the present anti-slavery agitation began, by a northern Methodist preacher, who, while residing at the south, had an opportunity to see slaveholding morals, manners, and piety, with his own eyes. "Shall I not visit for these things? saith the Lord. Shall not my soul be avenged on such a nation as this?"

A PARODY.*

Come, saints and sinners, hear me tell
How pious priests whip Jack and Nell,
And women buy and children sell,

---

*This is a parody of "Heavenly Union," a hymn popular in the South.

And preach all sinners down to hell,
  And sing of heavenly union.

They'll bleat and baa, dona like goats,
Gorge down black sheep, and strain at motes,
Array their backs in fine black coats,
Then seize their negroes by their throats,
  And choke, for heavenly union.

They'll church you if you sip a dram,
And damn you if you steal a lamb;
Yet rob old Tony, Doll, and Sam,
Of human rights, and bread and ham;
  Kidnapper's heavenly union.

They'll loudly talk of Christ's reward,
And bind his image with a cord,
And scold, and swing the lash abhorred,
And sell their brother in the Lord
  To handcuffed heavenly union.

They'll read and sing a sacred song,
And make a prayer both loud and long,
And teach the right and do the wrong,
Hailing the brother, sister throng,
  With words of heavenly union.

We wonder how such saints can sing,
Or praise the Lord upon the wing,
Who roar, and scold, and whip, and sting,
And to their slaves and mammon* cling,
  In guilty conscience union.

They'll raise tobacco, corn, and rye,
And drive, and thieve, and cheat, and lie,
And lay up treasures in the sky,

*Wealth regarded as an evil influence.

By making switch and cowskin fly,
 In hope of heavenly union.

They'll crack old Tony on the skull,
And preach and roar like Bashan bull,
Or braying ass, of mischief full,
Then seize old Jacob by the wool,
 And pull for heavenly union.

A roaring, ranting, sleek man-thief,
Who lived on mutton, veal, and beef,
Yet never would afford relief
To needy, sable sons of grief,
 Was big with heavenly union.

'Love not the world,' the preacher said,
And winked his eye, and shook his head;
He seized on Tom, and Dick, and Ned,
Cut short their meat, and clothes, and bread,
 Yet still loved heavenly union.

Another preacher whining spoke
Of One whose heart for sinners broke:
He tied old Nanny to an oak,
And drew the blood at every stroke,
 And prayed for heavenly union.

Two others oped their iron jaws,
And waved their children-stealing paws;
There sat their children in gewgaws;
By stinting negroes' backs and maws,
 They kept up heavenly union.

All good from Jack another takes,
And entertains their flirts and rakes,
Who dress as sleek as glossy snakes,
And cram their mouths with sweetened cakes;
 And this goes down for union.

Sincerely and earnestly hoping that this little book may do something toward throwing light on the American slave system, and has-
tening the glad day of deliverance to the millions of my brethren in
bonds—faithfully relying upon the power of truth, love, and justice,
for success in my humble efforts—and solemnly pledging my self
anew to the sacred cause,—I subscribe myself,

Frederick Douglass.
Lynn, Mass., April 28, 1845.

ENDNOTES

1. (p. 3) *having recently made his escape from the southern prison-house of bondage:* On September 3, 1838, Douglass (then Frederick Bailey) escaped from slavery; he traveled north from Baltimore, Maryland, and settled in New Bedford, Massachusetts, where he became active in the abolition movement.

2. (p. 3) *"gave the world assurance of a MAN":* Garrison is quoting from a passage in William Shakespeare's *Hamlet*, in which Hamlet describes his father: "A combination and a form indeed, / Where every god did seem to set his seal / To give the world assurance of a man" (act 3, scene 4).

3. (p. 3) *I shall never forget his first speech at the convention:* The Massachusetts Anti-Slavery Convention was held on the island of Nantucket in 1841, from August 10 to August 12. Note also in this paragraph that Garrison's description of Douglass exemplifies how, as a former slave, he would be presented by the abolitionists as an exhibit and "an ornament."

4. (p. 4) *by the terms of the slave code:* The slave codes, different in each state, were laws pertaining to the legal status of slaves and free blacks. They included punishments for such crimes as murder and arson as well as insolence toward and association with whites; punishments ranged from branding or whipping to death.

5. (p. 4) *A beloved friend from New Bedford:* Garrison is referring to William C. Coffin, a leading antislavery activist in New Bedford when Douglass moved there in 1838.

6. (p. 4) *PATRICK HENRY, of revolutionary fame:* Patrick Henry (1736–1799) was a Virginia-born American Revolutionary leader, an orator, and a politician. Henry is renowned for his saying "Give me liberty, or give me death," delivered in a convention speech in 1775; Douglass alludes to these famous words in his *Narrative* (see p. 79).

7. (p. 5) *John A. Collins: Collins* (1810–1879) was an abolitionist and reformer and a member of the Massachusetts Anti-Slavery Society; he resigned from the Society in 1843.

8. (p. 6) *Charles Lenox Remond:* Born in Massachusetts to free parents, Remond (1810–1873) became an agent of the Massachusetts Anti-Slavery Society in 1838; he was the first African American employed by the Society as a lecturer. During the Civil War, Remond recruited soldiers for the Fifty-fourth Massachusetts Volunteers infantry. He later clerked in the Boston Custom House.

9. (p. 6) *Daniel O'Connell:* Known as the Liberator, Daniel O'Connell (1775–1847) was an Irish nationalist leader who fought for Catholic emancipation and Irish independence; O'Connell toured with Douglass in 1842.

10. (p. 8) *SLAVERY AS IT IS:* Here and throughout this paragraph, Garrison offers a guarantee of the authenticity of Douglass's report on slavery in terms that were typical of white abolitionists' prefaces to slave narratives. The phrase "slavery as it is" may refer to Theodore Weld's *American Slavery As It Is: Testimony of a Thousand Witnesses* (New York: The American Anti-Slavery Society, 1839), a best-selling compilation of reports in southern newspapers of brutalities suffered by slaves.

11. (p. 11) *"NO COMPROMISE WITH SLAVERY! NO UNION WITH SLAVEHOLDERS!":* Garrison's flourish at the end of the preface echoes the rhetoric of the exhortatory abolitionist speech.

12. (p. 13) *In 1838, many were waiting for the results of the West India experiment:* This is a reference to the emancipation of all slaves in the British West Indies; the process began with the Abolition Act of 1833, which called for abolishing slavery throughout the British Empire, and was peacefully completed on August 1, 1838.

13. (p. 17) *I have no accurate knowledge of my age, never having seen any authentic record containing it:* Evidence that was unavailable to Douglass indicates he was born in February 1818, and that he was twenty-seven years old while writing this *Narrative*. The question of his correct birth date and age plagued Douglass through his life.

14. (p. 17) *My father was a white man:* Circumstantial and inconclusive evidence suggests that Douglass's father was either Aaron Anthony, manager of the plantation Douglass was born on, or Thomas Auld, Anthony's son-in-law.

15. (p. 19) *it will do away the force of the argument, that God cursed Ham:* Noah's punishment of his son Ham (which was to pronounce Ham's son Canaan a slave to his brothers; see the Bible, Genesis 9:20–27) has been used to justify racism and prejudice against peoples of African descent, as some of Ham's descendants, notably Cush, are black.

16. (p. 20) *Colonel Lloyd:* Edward Lloyd V (1779–1834) was a governor of Maryland, a U.S. senator, and a slaveholder.

17. (p. 23) *If a slave was convicted of any high misdemeanor, . . . he was . . . sold to Austin Woolfolk, or some other slave-trader:* Before Douglass had reached the age of fourteen, one of his sisters, two aunts, seven cousins, and at least five other relatives, as well as other slaves he knew well, were sold farther south, many of them by the notorious Baltimore slave trader Austin Woolfolk.

18. (p. 24) *Mr. Severe was rightly named:* Throughout his *Narrative*, Douglass is careful to give the actual names of all the individuals he mentions; he is just as careful to emphasize the irony of a name like this one (and Mr. Gore, Mr. Freeland, and others). In this case, Douglass has the local pronunciation (and thus its irony) correct, but the actual spelling was "Sevier"; an overseer on Lloyd's plantation, William Sevier had control over 165 slaves.

19. (p. 28) *The colonel also kept a splendid riding equipage. His stable and carriage-house presented the appearance of some of our large city livery establishments. . . . His carriage-house contained . . . three or four gigs, besides dearborns and barouches of the most fashionable style:* Douglass is comparing the colonel's riding equipage his carriages and horses—to the city's large commercial stables, known as livery establishments. Gigs are light, two-wheeled carriages drawn by one horse; dearborns are light, four-wheeled carriages with curtained sides; and barouches are four-wheeled carriages with a covered passenger area that has facing double seats.

20. (p. 29) *enjoyed the luxury of whipping the servants when they pleased:* Here and elsewhere Douglass's sarcasm is very sharp concerning the sadistic nature of slavery's systems of control.

21. (p. 36) *My feet have been so cracked with the frost, that the pen with which I am writing might be laid in the gashes:* Douglass uses this powerful literary device—in which the writer's physical response or demonstration adds weight to a memory of the past—several times. See, for another example, the end of chapter II (p. 26), where he reports that as he was writing "an expression of feeling has already found its way down my cheek."

22. (p. 37) *I spent most of all these three days in the creek, . . . preparing myself for my departure:* Douglass's attention to washing implies a ritual cleansing or baptism as he prepares for a new life in the celebrated city of Baltimore.

23. (p. 41) *Baltimore:* Baltimore had one of the largest concentrations of free people of color in the South; the free black community was nearly 30,000 strong.

24. (p. 43) *Slavery proved as injurious to her as it did to me:* One of the themes in Douglass's *Narrative* is that slavery was ruinous to all participants, black and white, slave and slaveholder.

25. (p. 45) *Just about this time, I got hold of a book entitled "The Columbian Orator":* Caleb Bingham edited *The Columbian Orator: Containing a Variety of Original and Selected Pieces Together with Rules Calculated to Improve Youth and Others in the Ornamental and Useful Art of Eloquence.* First published in 1797, this anthology contained speeches dating from classical antiquity through the American Revolution and featured passage after passage about freedom, democracy, and courage—including the crucial "Dialogue Between a Master and Slave." In addition, there was an extensive preface by Bingham on public speaking. Douglass bought a secondhand copy of the anthology for fifty cents at a bookstore on Thames Street, Baltimore. In preparation for his role in the abolition movement and as a spokesman for justice and freedom, Douglass could hardly have purchased a better guide and source book.

26. (p. 45) *one of Sheridan's mighty speeches on and in behalf of Catholic emancipation:* Douglass is referring here not to the speeches of Richard Brinsley Sheridan (1751–1816), the Irish political leader and dramatist, but to the "Speech in the Irish House of Commons in Favour of the Bill for Emancipating the Roman Catholics, 1795," by the Irish patriot Arthur O'Connor.

27. (p. 46) *If a slave . . . did any thing very wrong in the mind of a slaveholder, it was spoken of as the fruit of abolition:* It is likely that thirteen-year-old Douglass first read about "abolitionists" in the *Baltimore American* in August 1831, when Nat Turner's slave rebellion in Virginia was front-page news.

28. (p. 51) *she saw her children, her grandchildren, and her great-grandchildren, divided, like so many sheep:* It turns out that Douglass was mistaken in his accusations against Thomas Auld regarding his grandmother's treatment. In fact, after Betsey Bailey's husband, Isaac, died Auld took her in and cared for her until her death in 1849. In a letter published in the *North Star* on September 7, 1849, Douglass apologized to Auld for the misstatement; he did so again during his famous meeting with Auld in June 1877, as Auld was dying.

29. (p. 52) *St. Michael's:* It was on this neck of land between the Miles and Broad Rivers that many of the clippers that established Baltimore as a major port city were produced.

30. (p. 56) *I have also seen Mr. George Cookman at our house. We slaves loved Mr. Cookman:* George Cookman was a Methodist minister, twice chaplain to the House of Representatives.

31. (pp. 63–64) *I would pour out my soul's complaint, in my rude way, with an apostrophe to the moving multitude of ships:—"You are loosed from your moorings, and are free; I am fast in my chains, and am a slave! . . . There is a better day coming":* This apostrophe (a rhetorical address to a personified thing) echoes the biblical lament of Job when he speaks "in the bitterness of [his] soul" (see the Bible, Job 7:11, 10:1; King James Version); it ends with a line found in many Negro spirituals, "There's a better day a-coming." Perhaps the passage contains something of the teenager's voice as well.

32. (p. 67) *I found Sandy an old adviser:* Here "old" implies ancient wisdom won through long-cultivated experience and, perhaps, a connection with African traditions. The man's name, Sandy, also may imply a connection between the natural and the spiritual realms.

33. (p. 71) *The holidays are part and parcel of the gross fraud, wrong, and inhumanity of slavery. . . . So, when the holidays ended, we staggered up . . . feeling, upon the whole, rather glad to go . . . back to the arms of slavery:* This passage on drunkenness during the holidays typifies the abolitionist-temperance rhetoric of the time. Note how elsewhere in this book the slaveholders' extravagances of injustice are often enflamed by their drunkenness.

34. (p. 79) *I was never more certain of any thing:* Here again—as in the incident with the root (pp. 67–68)—Sandy's extraordinary powers are displayed; and again Douglass shares with him an experience of such powers.

35. (p. 81) *"You yellow devil. . . . you long-legged mulatto devil!":* The theme of miscegenation (mixing of races) runs throughout the *Narrative.* Douglass knows his father is a white man; he observes that the white masters' illicit slave children—a reproach to the white men's wives—are sometimes singled out for special mistreatment (p. 19); here Douglass himself is vilified in terms that recall racist typologies concerning the peculiarly dangerous character of people of mixed race.

36. (p. 81) *"Own nothing!":* Note that this advice follows several other examples of Douglass's lesson that silence is often the best defense: "A still tongue makes a wise head" (p. 30).

37. (p. 85) *to strike a white man is death by Lynch law:* The phrase "lynch law" refers to the punishment, usually by execution, of an accused person without legal procedure or authority. Lynch law was part of the slave codes (see note 4, above).

38. (p. 88) underground railroad: This term describes the abolition movement's practice of assisting fugitive slaves in their escape from the South to the free North and West.

39. (p. 94) *I was relieved . . . by the humane hand of MR. DAVID RUGGLES:* An African American born free in Connecticut, David Ruggles (1810–1849) founded the New York Vigilance Committee, an organization that helped fugitive slaves escape slavery. He aided Douglass in his escape from Maryland, and permitted Douglass to stay in his home on his way to New Bedford in 1838.

40. (p. 94) *Mr. Ruggles was then very deeply engaged in the memorable* Darg *case:* On September 6, 1839, Ruggles was arrested for harboring Thomas Hughes, a fugitive slave from Arkansas who was pursued by his owner John P. Darg.

41. (p. 94) *Anna, my intended wife:* Douglass met Anna Murray (1813–1882), a free black and an abolitionist, in Baltimore. She sold one of her two featherbeds to help Douglass pay for his escape, and later joined him in New York. She and Douglass were married for forty-four years and raised five children.

42. (p. 95) *"J. W. C. Pennington":* After escaping from slavery in Maryland around 1831, Pennington (1807–1870) went on to teach, write, and speak against slavery, and to pastor Congregational and Presbyterian churches. He wrote *The Fugitive Blacksmith; or, Events in the history of James W. C. Pennington, pastor of a Presbyterian church, New York, formerly a slave in the State of Maryland* (London, 1850).

43. (p. 96) *Mr. Johnson had just been reading the "Lady of the Lake," and at once suggested that my name be "Douglass":* The name "Douglas," to which Douglass added an *s*, is from Sir Walter Scott's 1810 poem *Lady of the Lake*, a historical romance set in the Scottish Highlands. Scott's Lord James of Douglas is a wrongfully exiled Scottish chieftain, revered for his goodness and bravery. This whole paragraph, which deals with names and naming, is quite significant in a context in which slaves in America could not be sure of their ancestry, or sometimes even—as in the case of Douglass—of their father's identity. From the slave narratives through *The Autobiography of Malcolm X* (1965), this problem of names has reflected larger problems of identity and familial linkage: the sometimes heroic, sometimes blundering and comic, quest for home and family in a world where one's name is invented, one's identity an improvisation.

44. (p. 96) *I was quite disappointed at the general appearance of things in New Bedford:* By "disappointed," Douglass means "unsettled" or "surprised"; the reality of life in New Bedford was much more orderly and prosperous than the southern planters would have had Douglass believe to be the case in the free North.

45. (p. 100) *Never was there a clearer case of "stealing the livery of the court of heaven to serve the devil in":* Douglass is recalling lines from *The Course of Time*, by Scottish poet Robert Pollok (1799–1827): "He was a man / Who stole the livery of the court of Heaven / To serve the Devil in" (book 8, lines 616–618).

46. (p. 102) *Pilate and Herod friends!:* Pontius Pilate was the Roman procurator of

Judea (26–c.36 A.D.) who tried and condemned Jesus. Herod I (known as Herod the Great) was the Roman-appointed king of Judea (37–4 B.C.) when Jesus was born; in the Bible, Herod is responsible for the extermination of infants of Bethlehem (Matthew 2:16–18).

INSPIRED BY *NARRATIVE OF THE LIFE OF FREDERICK DOUGLASS, AN AMERICAN SLAVE*

America has the mournful honor of adding a new department to the literature of civilization,—the autobiographies of escaped slaves.

—Ephraim Peabody

Slave Narratives

The autobiographical slave narrative is a specific literary genre that includes works from as long ago as the early 1700s. *A Narrative of the Uncommon Sufferings and Surprizing Deliverance of Briton Hammon, a Negro Man* (1760) is generally considered the first slave narrative, although *Adam Negro's Tryall* appeared in 1703. The age of *Robinson Crusoe*-type adventure tales included several chronicles of slavery, among them *A Narrative of the Lord's Wonderful Dealings with J. Murrant, a Black, Taken Down from His Own Relation* (1784) and *The Interesting Narrative of Olaudah Equiano, or Gustavus Vassa, the African* (1789). *The History of Mary Prince: A West Indian Slave*, the first slave narrative written by a woman, was published in 1831.

But slave narratives did not gel as a literary form until 1845, when Frederick Douglass published his story. His articulate descriptions of the abuses perpetrated by his masters revealed horrors of slavery that previously were unimaginable to most Americans and spurred a nation-wide public outrage against slavery.

Douglass's narrative was followed by more slaves' stories, including *Incidents in the Life of a Slave Girl* (1861), published under the pseudonym Linda Brent; the author was actually Harriet Jacobs, an escaped slave who worked for a time with Douglass's circle of abolitionists in Rochester, New York. Harriet Tubman led so many slaves to freedom as a "conductor" of the Underground Railroad that she earned the nickname "Moses." Unable to read or write, Tubman dictated her 1869 narrative, *Scenes in the Life of Harriet Tubman*.

Slave narratives not only gave voice to many African Americans, who were previously excluded from the literary life of the nation; they also left their mark on modern literature. For example, describing her aim in writing the novel *Beloved* (1987), Toni Morrison said she wished "to fill in the blanks that the slave narratives left, to part the veil that was so frequently drawn." *Beloved*, which includes descriptions of the Middle Passage (the delivery of Africans on ships to the Americas) and the Underground Railroad, earned Morrison a Pulitzer Prize in 1988.

Visual Art

One of the most highly regarded artists of the twentieth century, Jacob Lawrence (1917–2000) produced a huge body of work. After attending Frederick Douglass Junior High School in New York City, Lawrence began forging his identity as a modern artist and became associated with the Harlem Renaissance in its later stages. Later, almost echoing Douglass's ideas, Lawrence said, "My belief is that it is most important for an artist to develop an approach and philosophy about life—if he has developed this philosophy, he does not put paint on canvas, he puts himself on canvas." When he was twenty-two, Lawrence painted a series of thirty-two panels titled *The Life of Frederick Douglass*. Executed in a simple, allegorical style and striking, vibrant colors, the panels depict many of the events Douglass describes in his Narrative—learning to read, resisting the slave-breaker Mr. Covey, planning his escape, listening to William Lloyd Garrison lecture in the North, and receiving government appointments.

Children's Literature

A civil-rights activist, distinguished actor, accomplished director, and published author, Ossie Davis personifies the achievement Frederick Douglass sought for African Americans. Davis wrote and directed *Escape to Freedom: The Story of Young Frederick Douglass* (1978), a chronicle of Douglass's early life through his escape to the North. The play educates children on Douglass's many accomplishments, including his books, speeches, and political appointments. Davis has been honored with the NAACP Image Award, the National Medal of Arts, the Screen Actors Guild Life Achievement Award, and the New York Urban League Frederick Douglass Award.

Statuary

Frederick Douglass was the first African American to whom a public sculpture was dedicated. The bronze statue was dedicated on June 9, 1899, in Rochester, New York, with Theodore Roosevelt, governor of New York, in attendance. The cast of Douglass stands with arms held forward, palms up, as if welcoming visitors. The statue is the work of James W. Thomas, an African-American artist from Rochester. Originally erected near the train station, the statue enjoyed a prominent position in the city; in 1941 it was moved to Highland Park, near the site of Douglass's Rochester home.

COMMENTS & QUESTIONS

In this section, we aim to provide the reader with an array of perspectives on the text, as well as questions that challenge those perspectives. The commentary has been culled from sources as diverse as reviews contemporaneous with the work, letters written by the author, literary criticism of later generations, and appreciations written throughout the work's history. Following the commentary, a series of questions seeks to filter Narrative of the Life of Frederick Douglass, an American Slave *through a variety of voices and bring about a richer understanding of this enduring work.*

Comments

LYNN PIONEER

My readers will be delighted to learn that Frederick Douglass—the fugitive slave—has at last concluded his narrative. All who know the wonderful gifts of friend Douglass know that his narrative must, in the nature of things, be written with great power. It is so indeed. It is the most thrilling work which the American press ever issued—*and the most important.* If it does not open the eyes of this people, they must be petrified into eternal sleep.

The picture it presents of slavery is too horrible to look upon, and yet it is but a faint *picture* of what to millions is a vivid *life.* It is evidently drawn with a nice eye, and the coloring is chaste and subdued, rather than extravagant or overwrought. Thrilling as it is, and full of the most burning eloquence, it is yet simple and touching as the impulses of childhood. There are passages in it which would brighten the reputation of any living author,—while the book, as a whole, judged as a mere work of art would widen the fame of Bunyan or De Foe. A spirit of the loftiest integrity, and a vein of the purest religious sentiment, runs through its pages, and it must leave on every mind a deep conviction of the author's strength of mind and purity of heart. I predict for it a sale of at least twenty thousand in this country, and equally great in Europe. It will leave a mark upon this age which the

busy finger of time will deepen at every touch. It will generate a public sentiment in this nation, in the presence of which our pro-slavery
laws and constitutions shall be like chaff in the presence of fire. It
contains the spark which will kindle up the smoldering embers of
freedom in a million souls, and light up our whole continent with the
flames of liberty. Great efforts will be made in the name of the Constitution and the Bible, of James Polk and the Apostle Paul, to suppress it; but it will run through this nation from house to house, and
from heart to heart, as the wild fire, *finding wings in every wind which
blows*, flies across the tall and boundless prairies. Its stirring incidents
will fasten themselves on the eager minds of the youth of this country with hooks of steel. The politics of the land will stand abashed before it, while her more corrupt religion will wish to sink back into the
hot womb which gave it birth. It will fall in among the churches and
state-houses of the land like a bomb-shell.

—from *The Liberator* (May 30, 1845)

MARGARET FULLER

Frederick Douglass has been for some time a prominent member of
the Abolition party. He is said to be an excellent speaker—can speak
from a thorough personal experience—and has upon the audience,
beside, the influence of a strong character and uncommon talents.
In the book before us he has put into the story of his life the
thoughts, the feelings, and the adventures that have been so affecting
through the living voice; nor are they less so from the printed page.
He has had the courage to name the persons, times and places, thus
exposing himself to obvious danger, and setting the seal on his deep
convictions as to the religious need of speaking the whole truth.
Considered merely as a narrative, we have never read one more simple, true, coherent, and warm with genuine feeling. It is an excellent
piece of writing, and on that score to be prized as a specimen of the
powers of the Black Race, which Prejudice persists in disputing. We
prize highly all evidence of this kind, and it is becoming more abundant. . . .

The book is prefaced by two communications—one from Garrison and one from Wendell Phillips. That from the former is in his
usual over-emphatic style. His motives and his course have been
noble and generous. We look upon him with high respect, but he has

indulged in violent invective and denunciation till he has spoiled the
temper of his mind. Like a man who has been in the habit of scream-
ing himself hoarse to make the deaf better, he can no longer pitch his
voice on a key agreeable to common ears. Mr. Phillips's remarks are
equally decided, without the exaggeration in the tone. Douglass himself seems very just and temperate. We feel that his view, even of
those who have injured him most, may be relied upon. He knows
how to allow for motives and influences. Upon the subject of Religion, he speaks with great force, and not more than our own sympathies can respond to. The inconsistencies of Slaveholding professors
of religion cry to Heaven. We are not disposed to detest, or refuse
communion with them. Their blindness is but one form of that
prevalent fallacy which substitutes a creed for a faith, a ritual for a
life. We have seen too much of this system of atonement not to know
that those who adopt it often began with good intentions, and are, at
any rate, in their mistakes worthy of deepest pity. But that is no reason why the truth should not be uttered, trumpet-tongued, about the
thing. "Bring no more vain oblations": sermons must daily be
preached anew on that text. Kings, five hundred years ago, built
Churches with the spoils of war; Clergymen today command Slaves
to obey a Gospel which they will not allow them to read, and call
themselves Christians amid the curses of their fellow men. The world
ought to get on a little faster than that, if there be really any principle of movement in it. The Kingdom of Heaven may not at the beginning have dropped seed larger than a mustard seed, but even from
that we had a right to expect a fuller growth than can be believed to
exist, when we read such a book as this of Douglass. . . .

We wish that every one may read his book and see what a mind
might have been stifled in bondage—what a man may be subjected
to the insults of spendthrift dandies, or the blows of mercenary
brutes, in whom there is no whiteness except of the skin, no humanity except in the outward form, and of whom the Avenger will not
fail yet to demand—"Where is thy brother?"

—from the *New York Tribune* (June 10, 1845)

NATIONAL ANTI-SLAVERY STANDARD
We had a book put into our hands the other day, purporting to be the
autobiography of a slave, who had escaped from bondage, by the

name of Frederick Douglass, and we frankly acknowledge, that had
it not been for our confidence in the good judgment of the friend
from whom the book came, who we knew had little sympathy with
the class of technical Abolitionists, we might possibly have laid it
aside, without reading it, from perceiving that it was published under
the patronage of several individuals, whose course on the subject of
Slavery we have never regarded as either politic or right.

On looking into the book, however, we have found it to contain
one of the most remarkable and thrilling narratives that have ever
fallen under our eye; and though there are some things in it which we
regret, particularly the strong expressions against professing Christians at the South, yet we see nothing to cast even a shade of doubt
over the authenticity of the narrative, even in respect to its minutest
details. We should indeed, have made a single exception to this remark—that is, we should have doubted the practicability of such a
book being produced by a poor runaway slave, had it not been that
we are assured that his efforts as a public speaker are quite equal to
what he has here shown himself to be as a writer; and we have it upon
good authority, that his lectures are characterized by as able reasoning, as genuine wit, and as bold and stirring appeals, as we almost
ever find in connection with the highest intellectual culture.

Unless we greatly mistake, this small work to which we are referring is destined to exert a mighty influence in favor of the great cause
of Emancipation. We acknowledge for ourselves, that we might have
heard the system of Slavery reasoned against abstractly, no matter
how ably, and no matter how long, and yet we could not have been
so deep impressed with it as an outrage against humanity, as we have
been by reading this simple story. It is especially fitted to correct a too
prevalent error that Slavery *in itself* is not deserving of any severe
reprobation—that it is only the abuses of the system with which we
have a right to find fault.

And we acknowledge ourselves to be among those who look for
its removal at no distant day. It seems to us as clear as the shining of
the sun, that there are signs of the times which betoken a speedy and
mighty revolution on this subject. The march of public opinion is evidently in favor of emancipation; and opposition can no more arrest
it than it can arrest the motion of the planets. There is a spirit awake
throughout all the North, that cries out for universal Freedom, and

all the agitation and opposition that we witness at the South is but the heaving of the same spirit under different circumstances. It tells of a terrible conflict between selfishness and conscience, which will certainly terminate at last in favor of the better principle.

What particular mode of abolishing Slavery from our land, Providence may ordain—whether it shall be by bringing the South to bow to the high dictates of conscience and of duty, or by suffering the slaves themselves to become ministers of vengeance toward their oppressors, or by some other means, of which we know nothing—we pretend not to say; but the event of ultimate emancipation, in some way, we consider as absolutely certain; and while we would have all labor to bring it about, we would have all take counsel of the spirit of prudence, as well as philanthropy, in respect to the channel in which their labors shall be directed.

—August 7, 1845

EPHRAIM PEABODY
The narrative of Douglass contains the life of a superior man. Since his escape from slavery, he has been employed as an antislavery lecturer, and is now the editor of a newspaper in Rochester, N.Y. He does not belong to the class, always small, of those who bring to light great principles, or who originate new methods of carrying them out. He has, however, the vividness of sensibility and of thought which we are accustomed to associate with a Southern climate. He has a natural and ready eloquence, a delicacy of taste, a quick perception of properties, a quick apprehension of ideas, and a felicity of expression, which are possessed by few among the more cultivated, and which are surprising when we consider that it is but a few years since he was a slave. In any popular assembly met for the discussion of subjects with which he has had the opportunity to become familiar, he is a man to command and hold attention. He is a natural orator, and his original endowments and the peculiarity of his position have given him a high place among antislavery speakers.

But while our sympathies go strongly with him, and because they go with him, we are disposed to make a criticism on a mode of address in which he sometimes indulges himself, which we believe is likely to diminish, not only his usefulness, but his real influence. We would not detract from his merits, and we can easily excuse in him a

severity of judgment and a one-sidedness of view which might be in-
excusable in another. We can hardly condemn one who has been a
slave for seeing only the evils of slavery, and for thinking lightly of
the difficulty of remedying them; but we have wished, when we have
heard him speak, or read what he has written, that he might wholly
avoid a fault from which a natural magnanimity does something towards saving him, but to which he is nevertheless exposed. His asso-
ciates at the North have been among those who are apt to mistake
violence and extravagance of expression and denunciation for eloquence;—men who, whatever their virtues otherwise, are not in the
habit of using discrimination to their judgments of men or of measures which they do not approve. To him they have doubtless been
true and faithful friends, and he naturally adopts their style of speech.
But it is a mistaken one, if the speaker wishes to sway the judgment
of his hearers and to accomplish any practical end. No matter what
the vehemence of tone or expression, whenever a public speaker indulges himself in violent and unqualified statements and in sweeping
denunciations, he not only makes it apparent that he is deficient in a
sound and fair judgment, but what is worse, he creates in his hearers
a secret distrust of his real earnestness,—a vague feeling that after all
he is thinking more of his speech than of the end for which he pro-
fesses to make it. When men are profoundly in earnest, they are not
apt to be extravagant. The more earnest, the more rigidly true. A
merchant, in discussing the politics of the day, about which he knows
or cares little, freely indulges in loose, extravagant, and violent declarations. But follow him to his counting-room; let him be making inquiries or giving directions about some enterprise which he really has
deeply at heart, and the extravagance is gone. Nothing will answer
here but truth, and the exact truth. His earnestness makes him calm.
It is seen in the moderated accuracy, as well as in the decision and
strength, of his statements. Extravagance and passion and rhetorical
flourishes might do when nothing which he greatly valued was at
stake; but here is something too serious for trifling. Just so it is in
other cases. A flippant, extravagant speaker, especially if he be gifted
with the power of sarcasm, will probably be listened to and ap-
plauded, but nothing comes of it. They who applaud the most understand very well that this is not the kind of person whose judgment
is to be relied on as a guide in action. His words are listened to with

much the same sort of interest that is given to the personated passion of the theatre. A few sober words from a calm, wise, discriminating mind are, after all, the ones which are followed. Nothing is less effective, for any practical end, than the "withering and scorching" eloquence with which American speeches seem so to abound. It conciliates no opponent, and though it may light up the momentary passions, it gives no new strength of conviction to the friends of a cause. It is the last kind of eloquence to be cultivated by those who are heartily in earnest in their desire to promote any great reform.

—from the *Christian Examiner* (July 1849)

BENJAMIN BRAWLEY
At the time of his death in 1895 Douglass had won for himself a place of unique distinction. Large of heart and of mind, he was interested in every forward movement for his people; but his charity embraced all men and all races. His reputation was international, and to-day many of his speeches are to be found in the standard works on oratory . . .

In an address on the 7th of December, 1890, [Frederick Douglass] said:

"I have seen dark hours in my life, and I have seen the darkness gradually disappearing, and the light gradually increasing. One by one I have seen obstacles removed, errors corrected, prejudices softened, proscriptions relinquished, and my people advancing in all the elements that make up the sum of general welfare. I remember that God reigns in eternity, and that, whatever delays, disappointments, and discouragements may come, truth, justice, liberty, and humanity will prevail."

—from *The Negro in Literature and Art* (1921)

Questions

1. Margaret Fuller distinguishes between overemphatic and temperate—or what may be termed preachy and reasoned—styles of address. Fuller finds Douglass to be of the temperate category. But Ephraim Peabody, a Unitarian minister, says Douglass is extravagant, which for Peabody indicates a lack of earnestness. Is Douglass preachy? Is there ever an occasion when preachiness might be the surest method of communication and, ultimately, the best way to win support?

2. At the end of the introduction to this volume Professor O'Meally argues that Frederick Douglass in his *Narrative* "was working those roots for reversals of ill fortune not just for himself, . . . but for us all." Do you agree? Is it possible that the *Narrative* might inspire anyone to throw off whatever chains bind him or her?

3. Douglass was long associated with the women's rights movement. He spoke at the first Women's Rights Convention in Seneca Falls, New York, in 1848, and he was friends with Susan B. Anthony and Elizabeth Cady Stanton. Is there evidence in the *Narrative* of Douglass's sympathy with the situation of American women?

4. Douglass learned that freedom could be attained through skill with words. Find a paragraph or two in the *Narrative* in which rhetoric seems to work exceptionally well. Why is it so effective?

FOR FURTHER READING

Andrews, William L. *To Tell a Free Story: The First Century of Afro-American Autobiography, 1760–1865.* Urbana: University of Illinois Press, 1986.

———, ed. *Critical Essays on Frederick Douglass.* Boston: G. K. Hall, 1991.

Baker, Houston A., Jr. *Blues, Ideology, and Afro-American Literature: A Vernacular Theory.* Chicago: University of Chicago Press, 1984.

Blassingame, John W., and John R. McKivigan, eds. *The Frederick Douglass Papers.* Series 1: Speeches, Debates, and Interviews. 5 vols. New Haven, CT: Yale University Press, 1979–1992.

Blight, David W. *Frederick Douglass' Civil War: Keeping Faith in Jubilee.* Baton Rouge: Louisiana State University Press, 1989.

Bontemps, Ama Wendell. *Free at Last: The Life of Frederick Douglass.* New York: Dodd, Mead, 1971.

Davis, Charles T. *Black Is the Color of the Cosmos: Essays on Afro-American Literature and Culture, 1942–1981.* Edited by Henry Louis Gates, Jr. New York: Garland Publishing, 1982.

Douglass, Frederick. *Frederick Douglass: Autobiographies: Narrative of the Life; My Bondage and My Freedom; Life and Times.* Edited by Henry Louis Gates, Jr. New York: Library of America, 1994.

Fisher, Dexter, and Robert B. Stepto, eds. *Afro-American Literature: The Reconstruction of Instruction.* New York: Modern Language Association of America, 1978.

Foner, Philip S. *Frederick Douglass, a Biography.* New York: Citadel Press, 1964.

Griffin, Farah Jasmine. *"Who Set You Flowin'?": The African-American Migration Narrative.* New York: Oxford University Press, 1995.

Huggins, Nathan Irvin. *Slave and Citizen: The Life of Frederick Douglass.* Edited by Oscar Handlin. Boston: Little, Brown, 1980.

Martin, Waldo E., Jr. *The Mind of Frederick Douglass.* Chapel Hill: University of North Carolina Press, 1984.

McFeely, William S. *Frederick Douglass.* New York: W. W. Norton, 1991.

Morrison, Toni. "Rootedness: The Ancestor as Foundation." In *Black Women Writers (1950–1980): A Critical Evaluation*, edited by Mari Evans. Garden City, NY: Anchor Press, 1984.

Murray, Albert. *The Omni-Americans: New Perspectives on Black Experience and American Culture.* New York: Outerbridge and Dienstfrey, 1970.

Preston, Dickson J. *Young Frederick Douglass: The Maryland Years.* Baltimore, MD: Johns Hopkins University Press, 1980.

Quarles, Benjamin. *Frederick Douglass.* 1968. Reprint: New York: Athenaeum, 1968.

Stephens, Gregory. *On Racial Frontiers: The New Culture of Frederick Douglass, Ralph Ellison, and Bob Marley.* Cambridge and New York: Cambridge University Press, 1999.

Sundquist, Eric J., ed. *Frederick Douglass: New Literary and Historical Essays.* Cambridge and New York: Cambridge University Press, 1990.